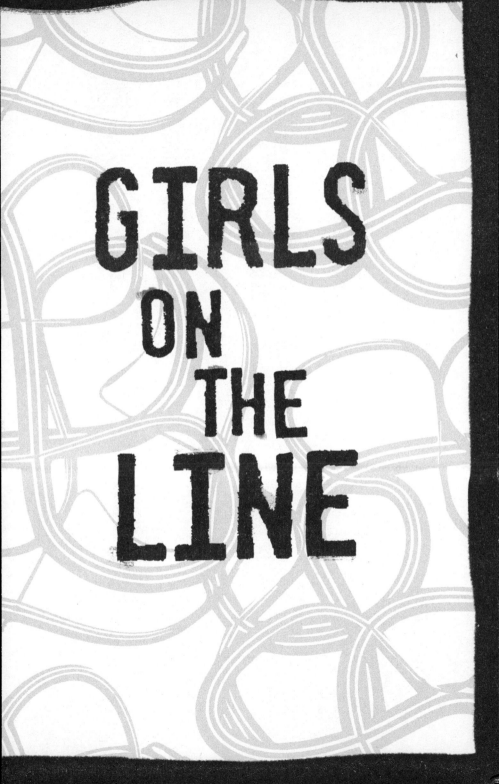

GIRLS ON THE LINE

GIRLS ON THE LINE

JENNIE LIU

carolrhoda LAB

MINNEAPOLIS

Carolrhoda Lab™
An imprint of Carolrhoda Books
A division of Lerner Publishing Group, Inc.
241 First Avenue North
Minneapolis, MN 55401 USA

For reading levels and more information, look up this title at www.lernerbooks.com.

Cover and interior images: Firsik/Shutterstock.com (abstract ink); foxie/Shutterstock.com (grungy frame); Parrot Ivan/Shutterstock.com (silhouette); Cartone Animato/Shutterstock.com (background circles).

Main body text set in Janson Text LT Std 10.5/15.
Typeface provided by Linotype AG.

Library of Congress Cataloging-in-Publication Data

Names: Liu, Jennie, 1971– author.
Title: Girls on the line / by Jennie Liu.
Description: Minneapolis : Carolrhoda Lab, [2018] | Summary: Told in two voices, Luli and Yun, raised in an orphanage to age sixteen, work together in a factory until Yun, pregnant, disappears and Luli must confront the dangers of the outside world to find her. Includes facts about China's One-Child Policy and its effects.
Identifiers: LCCN 2017031554| ISBN 9781512459388 (lb) | ISBN 9781541523760 (eb pdf)
Subjects: | CYAC: Missing persons—Fiction. | Factories—Fiction. | Pregnancy—Fiction. | Orphans—Fiction. | China—Fiction.
Classification: LCC PZ7.1.L5846 Gir 2018 | DDC [Fic]—dc23

LC record available at https://lccn.loc.gov/2017031554

Manufactured in the United States of America
1-43025-27694-6/15/2018

CHAPTER 1

Luli

The end-of-shift bell at Gujiao Technologies Limited rings out over the factory complex, the noise so shrill and piercing that I have to press my fingers against my ears. I stand on the outside of the retracting metal gate, waiting for Yun, while the guard strikes a match and lights a cigarette.

He has a thin moustache like a smear of dirt above his lip, and he leans against the gate near the sentry box blowing the smoke toward me. His eyes crawl over me, so I look away at everything else—the expanse of pavement between the white-tiled buildings, the people streaming in and out, the smokestacks spewing exhaust. The smog over Gujiao hides the late-day sun, and I wonder if the billowing vapor from the factory is what gives the hot air its chemical taste.

"Take one." The guard thrusts the pack of cigarettes toward me.

I glance at him from the corner of my eye and shake my head. My stomach feels full of moths, and his friendliness only makes me more uneasy.

He shrugs, taps out another cigarette, and lights it from the one burning down. "She won't get here for at least ten minutes. Building 8 is two blocks away. It's the biggest workroom.

She'll be ten minutes just getting out of the factory."

I bite my lip. The buildings are all identical, massive white-tiled structures standing neatly in line on either side of the long paved plaza, which itself is as wide as any avenue in the city. I scan the faces of the people flooding out of the buildings, searching for Yun. My eyes dart from one girl to another, and I realize that most of the workers are young, like Yun and me.

But not like me. These girls wear narrow jeans and tight-fitting tops, their hair falling sharply at angles or hanging long in ponytails, which bounce as they walk. Purses hang from their arms, and cell phones are clamped against their ears.

Yun has a cell phone now. She put the number in her letter and wrote that I could call her when I got here. She mentioned it so casually, as if I was the kind of person who could grab a phone and make a call. As if she's already forgotten what it's like to go out of the orphanage.

"She might have to do an overtime shift." The guard throws down his cigarette, pulls a cell phone out of his pocket, and begins staring at its screen. "Busy time for making the foreigners' things."

I anxiously squint at the faces on the other side of the gate. Yun did mention overtime in her letters, saying that it gives her extra money to buy snacks and clothes. And cell phones.

How long will I have to wait? I wonder how long an overtime shift lasts but don't want to ask the guard.

Several minutes pass. The crowd in the courtyard begins to thin as people move into other buildings. The guard lets a few workers out through the gate. They walk in groups of two or three with arms linked or huddled together, chatting and laughing, talking on their phones, some stopping to sit on the cement benches that line the avenue. The guard soon becomes busy opening and closing the gate as several more clusters of friends leave the complex. I move out of their way and turn to watch them going down the street.

A long time seems to have passed since the bell rang. My chest feels tight. If Yun doesn't show up, I don't know what I will do.

I think of the streets I walked to get here from the orphanage. They were choked with honking cars, six or seven alongside each other, and bicycles weaving among them. Smells of exhaust fought with scents of burning coal, fry oil, and urine. Huge glass-fronted department stores and office buildings towered over the streets and spanned entire blocks. People—many of them wearing masks against the pollution—went in every direction and jammed the sidewalks as they rushed to wherever they were going. I dodged them and tried to stay out of the way as I clutched Yun's letter with its scanty directions. It took me five hours to find my way across town.

I know I can't go back to the Institute, not as a ward, because I turned sixteen today and officially aged out. And the new worker started last week in the position they offered me. I wonder again, for the hundredth time, if I should have taken that job. I hoped for it for so long, even though I hated the Institute. It would have been at least a bed and work, rather than being thrust out alone.

But then Yun wrote offering to help me find work at the factory, and I nearly fell over with shock and relief. I'd been fascinated by her short letters about her new life, reading them over and over again, though I'd never thought of that kind of life for myself. Yet as soon as she said she would try to help me, I began to see myself working, making my own money, doing things with friends.

Now, still waiting at the gate, I'm terrified that I've made the wrong choice. The heat feels oppressive. The crowd begins to thin, and I still don't see her.

Someone starts waving. A girl in tight-fitting black pants and a shirt with yellow stripes is coming toward me. A wide, open-mouthed smile covers her face. She comes closer, and I see the black pockmarks on the right side of her face, the four unlucky marks the size of a pencil eraser that prevented her from being registered for adoption.

It's Yun. I swallow the lump in my throat, and I can breathe again.

"Open up!" Yun yells at the guard.

He pushes back the gate, and Yun grabs my arm and pulls me through into the complex.

"You made it!" Yun links her arm through mine and leads me along the avenue. "All done with that place!"

She's bubbling with energy, and all I can do is give a nervous smile. At the Institute, all the children were infected by the grim atmosphere. The caretakers often called Yun moody and picked on her even though she was a good worker. With the new clothes and shaggy haircut, she seems a different person. I feel shy with her.

She doesn't seem to notice and chatters on. "Did you have a hard time finding your way? I knew part of the way because I've gone around here lots of times, but I haven't been by the southern part of the city since I left the Institute." Her nose wrinkles up. "Oh! That place! How are the old caretakers?"

I try to think of something interesting to tell her, but nothing comes to mind. "The same."

Her expression flattens and she lets go my arm, looking suddenly like the Yun from the orphanage. Her eyes roam around the plaza, flicking from person to person as we thread through to wherever we're going.

I hurry after her, trying to stay close even though my feet hurt. My mind gropes for something to talk about that doesn't have to do with the Institute. "No overtime today? The guard said everyone was doing overtime."

"They told us we had to, but I said I was sick. First I held my stomach and bent over like I was having awful pains from my period. But the foreman didn't look like he was going to take the excuse, so I started coughing until he told me to go home." Yun covers her mouth and giggles, the new girl showing herself again. "Eat yet?" she asks.

I shake my head. I haven't eaten since the bowl of watery millet and vegetables I had before I left the Institute.

"Let's go have a snack. Did they give you any money?"

"No."

"Of course not. Doesn't matter. I'll pay for you. Let's go to my room and see if anyone can come with us."

I nod, though she's already pulling me along by the elbow through the factory complex. I'm happy to be led around.

We go by several buildings before entering Dorm Number 6. Inside, a dim corridor leads to the stairs at the other end. It looks much like the Institute with the long, dreary halls—except I hear music, laughter, and talking. When I peer into rooms with the doors propped open, I see brightly colored messes of clothes, stuffed animals, posters, and girls making themselves up or chatting on mobiles.

"You can share my bunk until you get a place," Yun says. "It's against the rules, but no one will find out. It's too late in the day to do anything about getting you a position right away. I'll talk to my foreman tomorrow—although maybe he isn't happy with me since I was sick today." She laughs. "Doesn't matter. It's easy to find work."

That's not what the caretakers told us. *No one wants to hire orphans.* Abandoned, never adopted, that's a curse no one wants around them. Here's Yun, though—showing that they were wrong.

Yun's room is on the fourth floor. The door is half closed, and she flings it open. Over her shoulder I can see four metal bunks on either side of the room, towels and clothing hanging from the posts, and lockers between them. A few of the beds have gauzy cloths strung up around them like curtains. A large window at the end of the room faces another building. Two girls huddled over a phone sit on a lower bunk with a rumpled yellow comforter.

"Anyone want to get something to eat?" Yun calls out.

Another girl lies reading on an upper bunk. She props up on an elbow, still holding the book. "Dining hall?"

Yun pulls a face and sticks out her tongue. "Yech! Why eat that junk? Not good enough for the dogs on the street. Let's go to the noodle shop or get hotpot."

"Dining hall is cheap," the other girl says. "I can't go spending all my wages eating out when the food is almost free here. I have to send money home." She flops back onto her pillow and goes back to reading.

Yun nudges me with her elbow. "The good thing about being an orphan. No one relying on you, asking you to send money home for medicine, for little brother's tuition, for adding a room onto the house." She turns to the other girls. "How about you, Hong and Zhenzhen? Want to come?"

Of the two girls sitting on the bunk, one has long hair and the other's is cut shoulder-length and shagged like Yun's. They both pull their faces away from the phone. "Okay."

They both get up and grab their purses, pulling out combs and lipstick.

Closing the door behind us, Yun points to the lower bunk behind it. "That one's mine. Put your stuff under there." She goes to her locker, takes off the lanyard that holds her work badge, and begins fixing herself up.

I stash the plastic bag that holds my few things under the bunk and sink down onto it. My legs are achy from the long walk. I'm exhausted, but at the same time I feel twitchy and excited.

The other girls are ready now and finally take notice of me. The one with long hair says, "What's your name?"

"Luli," I answer, then fall silent. I'm not used to talking to new people and don't know what more to say.

Yun says over her shoulder, "She's going to share my bunk until she gets a place."

The two girls glance at each other, then back at Yun, who's bent over and brushing her hair from the underside.

The reading girl props up onto her elbow again, then swings her legs over the side of the bunk. "If you're caught, you'll get fired. Or at least fined."

I look at Yun. I don't want her to get in trouble.

"We're not going to get caught." Yun talks from under her hair. "They never come around here. As long as no one reports us. I'm going to get her a place tomorrow." Still bending over, she tilts her head and starts brushing from the side. "She's from the orphanage. She doesn't have anyplace to go."

All the girls turn to me. Like with the guard, I can feel their eyes examining me, taking in the straight-chopped hair from the Institute, the thin shirt and pants that were given to me from donations. They're too big, and I've tied a rope around the waist.

"Do you have any other clothes?" Yun straightens up and flips her hair back.

"The shorts from the orphanage." The same ones all the orphans wear, the ones I've been wearing for years.

Yun wrinkles her nose and grimaces. "Doesn't matter. When you get your first pay you'll go shopping." She stuffs her hairbrush into a small purple knapsack and slings it over her shoulders. "Let's go."

Outside the factory gates Yun walks between Hong and Zhenzhen, discussing their bosses. They're in different departments. I try to follow the talk, but I'm tired. Tired from walking all day, the stress of trying to find this place, everything so different. Yun so different.

And I'm so hungry. Above all the smells of the city, the smells of food come to me, make my stomach tighten up like a fist. I'm excited about getting something to eat. Something other than millet soup with vegetables. I'm sure Yun is not going to take us to eat millet soup.

We pass through a couple of streets full of storefronts and littered with food stalls before coming to one lined with small restaurants. Yun ducks into one that's across the street from a dusty, unpaved lot with pool tables outside. Young men in their undershirts are leaning over the tables taking shots or smoking as they wait their turn.

In the restaurant, half a dozen tables are squeezed together with plastic stools under them. A TV on a high shelf in one corner is blaring *Justice Bao*, a serial the workers at the orphanage used to watch. Only two tables are occupied, one where three customers are hunched over bowls, and the other where a man and a woman strip greens and stare up at the show.

We move to a table near the window. The woman gets up

from the vegetables, comes over with a rag to swipe the table, and asks us what we want.

Yun orders: "Pork, long noodles, greens."

The woman nods and shouts at the man. He gets up slowly, eyes glued to the TV as he backs into the kitchen.

Of course, I've never eaten in a restaurant before, but Yun certainly has many times. She ordered so easily. As I watch her gossiping with her friends, her eyes flicking out the windows to the men across the street, I'm filled again with the feeling that she has changed so much. She and her friends sit chatting, and I can only watch them with nothing to say.

Yun interrupts Hong talking about her boyfriend to snap me out of my thoughts. "You look like you did the first day you came to the orphanage!"

I feel a flush come over the back of my neck. Out of place, yes.

Her voice softens. "Don't worry. You left that place. When you get a position, you'll be making money. You can eat anything you want! Buy clothes. Be your own person. No more taking care of babies, mopping floors, washing dishes."

I nod and try to smile, though my face feels stiff. Hong and Zhenzhen look back and forth between Yun and me. They don't know anything about what Yun was saying. They've probably never been in an orphanage.

"You can have a boyfriend." Zhenzhen elbows Hong, and all three girls bring their hands up to their mouths and giggle.

They keep it up until the woman comes over and plunks down bowls and a glass full of chopsticks. The cook follows with three steaming plates that he sets between us.

Such good smells rise up that my mouth begins to water. The noodles are broad and browned with soy. Hong draws them up in the air with her chopsticks and grabs my bowl to fill. The fatty meat is cut into little shreds, and the vegetable plate is full of greens glistening with oil. The girls pluck the meat and vegetables from the plates and scoop the noodles into their mouths from their bowls. The way Granddad and I used to eat before I went into the Institute. We didn't have food this rich, but I remember we ate like this, a few simple dishes set on the table. Not like at the Institute, lining up for a plop of soup every day.

The girls prattle on while they eat, but I only pay attention to my food until the high, nasal singing of a pop song comes out of nowhere. All three girls begin groping in their bags.

Yun shouts, "It's mine!" She pulls out her phone and begins talking very loudly while the rest of us openly listen. "Hey! Why so late? I thought you were going to meet me here. Where are you?" She listens for a moment, then stands up to look out the window across the street at the pool players. "I see you now." Listening again. "I have been looking for you, but I thought you said you would come to the restaurant. Doesn't matter. I'm coming now."

She clicks off and digs some cash out of her bag. "I have to go." She glances at me while counting out some bills. "Take this and pay for you and me. You can keep the rest in case you need anything. Pay me back once you've got a job." She thrusts the bills at me, and my hand moves automatically to take them. I'm dumbstruck that she's leaving. My stomach tightens.

Zhenzhen shoots Yun a sly smile. "So that was Yong calling you?"

Yun's already turning away from us. "I'll meet you back at the dorm," she calls over her shoulder as she rushes out of the restaurant.

Through the window I see her smoothing her hair as she crosses the street. She walks to the farthest pool table and leans against it as a guy in a snug black T-shirt takes a shot. He has sunglasses perched on his head, over hair that's greased and slicked back.

Hong and Zhenzhen are watching them as well. "Come on," says Hong. "Let's pay and go back to the dorm. She won't be back for hours."

CHAPTER 2

Yun

"Is that the girl you told me about?" Yong mutters through the cigarette clamped between his teeth. He stretches over the pool table, stares down his cue stick, and jerks his head toward the restaurant. "Your friend from the orphanage?"

I tear my eyes away from him to look across the street. The narrow restaurant is wedged between the Modern Women's Health Clinic and a row of clothing stalls, their metal doors rolled up and the shop owners hovering over the stray customers as they finger the bright rayon dresses and tables of socks.

Through the grimy window I can see the girls under the fluorescent light. I nod. "Luli." She's watching us, again with that same sad-eyed, scared look I remember from when we first met. From here, she could be eight years old. "She just went out today."

"You shouldn't have left her if she just got out." Yong takes his shot, then straightens up, swiping the sweat on his forehead up and back to his hair. He wears a close-fitting black T-shirt and jeans. It's easy to see the lean muscles on him as he walks around to the other side of the table.

I flush at the sting of his criticism and glance back at Luli. "I wanted to watch you play. Luli understands."

He shakes his head and gives a short laugh.

For a while we don't say anything. I lean against the table and watch Yong play against himself. The haze over the city is turning purple as dusk falls, but the air is still hot and humid. I flip my shirt to fan myself in the heat. When the only streetlight on this end of the road lights up, the noise from the guys at the other tables swells.

"What was it like there?" Yong asks. For a second, I don't know what he's talking about. I realize he means the Institute.

I shrug. I rarely think about it anymore.

"You never talk about it."

I wrinkle my face. "What's to say? I grew up there. It was all I knew." I start to pull on a thin lock of hair but catch myself and toss my head back, smiling. "I guess I didn't know anything then. Now, I see what I've been missing. Going out. Fun."

"Work."

"I knew about work. They taught us how to work there." I pick at some worn-out felt near a corner pocket of the table.

"What kind of work?"

"Mopping floors, doing wash, taking care of babies."

"Women's work."

I make a face at him.

"Sounds like it was easier than the factory."

I have to think about that. The work I do—hunched over the factory table full of charger cords for electronic cigarettes, winding them, then twisting a bit of plastic-wrapped wire around them—is mind-numbing, finger-numbing, neck- and back-aching. The days are so long. But I've gotten used to them.

I put my hands behind my head and stretch back against the stiffness in my body, the constant aches I've learned to ignore.

Yes, in a way, the work at the orphanage was easier because a person didn't have to do the same thing all day.

"Well, maybe. But I like making money. I would rather work and do what I want than still be living at the orphanage working with all those sad, sick little ones. I'm definitely better off now."

❖❖❖

I was nine and Luli was eight when she came to the Institute. Just out of the isolation period, she was brought into the dayroom. Her thin face and arms were tanned, which made me think she had come from the countryside. Her eyes moved across each child, the six or seven of us who were able-bodied enough to have free run of the room. First she looked at Guo, who stared back with his far-apart eyes. Then she gaped at the others, who shambled in their aimless courses around the room or rocked side to side on their haunches. When her dark pupils turned to me, I saw she was looking at my eyes instead of the pocks on my face. I was so surprised that I gaped at her as dully as the others until she dropped her gaze to the floor.

Caretaker Wong poked her head into the dayroom and shouted at me to start feeding the little ones. And to take the new girl along.

She followed me into the hall, and I asked her name. She didn't answer but studied her feet instead.

"I'm Yun." I said. I gave her a smile, which felt strange on my face. There wasn't much to smile about in the Institute.

She glanced at me again, then mumbled her name: "Luli."

I was pleased that she could speak. Most of the other older kids here couldn't really talk. "We big ones that are able have to work." I led her down the stairs to the kitchen. "We have to get the food now and help feed the little ones. Really, it's better than standing around all day. But it can be disgusting." Saying so much felt strange. There hadn't really been anyone to talk to for some time, at least no one who answered. "Nice to have someone to help me." I gave her another big, stiff smile over my shoulder as I grabbed two spoons and four bowls from a rack just inside the door.

"I don't know how to feed babies," she mumbled.

"Don't worry, it's not hard." I handed her two of the bowls, took two myself, and went over to the cook, who scooped millet and green vegetable porridge into them. I led her to the toddler room, where rows of cribs were crowded side by side.

"Just go around the room and give them each a bite."

She looked at the bowls in her hands and then around the room. The babies who were able were pulling themselves up to stand in their cribs. Some cried and reached out to us. Others just stood there.

"Come on. Hurry up." I grimaced. "I can't stand it when they start making so much noise."

We each put one of our bowls on the ground, and she watched me for a moment before she started. After she fed the first two babies, she began to talk to them with a sweet, whispery voice, but they just stared back. One shot her arm out to grab the bowl and nearly toppled it out of Luli's hands. She quickly learned to stay out of their reach, but she still grinned at them.

"How did you get here?" I asked.

The smile fell off her face. She fed another baby before she said anything. "Granddad's sick. Can't take care of me. Said I have to stay here until he gets better."

"Oh. Dying then."

She spun around with a wild look on her face. "He's just sick!"

I drew back at her shouting. Lots of times I'd seen kids come in when someone was too sick or too old to take care of them. They only left with new parents. "If he was going to get better, he wouldn't have sent you here," I said softly.

Her face turned to a terrible ruin. Her mouth pulled down and her eyes squeezed. It occurred to me that it was probably awful for her to hear these things. I groped for something else to say before she started crying. "At least they can't put you up for adoption until he dies. Unless he signed you away." I pulled another smile and gestured with my spoon for her to keep going with the food.

She stood for another moment staring at the bowl in her hands, but the babies were whimpering and demanding their food. We worked without talking for a while until she asked, "How long have you been here?"

"Since I was a baby. Left on the street near a grocery store. I was sick. Heart problem, and this." Still holding the spoon, I tapped the side of my face with the pocks.

"What do you mean?"

"Four black marks on my face. Unlucky four. Unlucky heart problem. No one wants unlucky. They won't even try getting the papers to put me up for adoption, not even to the foreigners."

Luli swung around again. "Foreigners?"

"When I was very little, there was a foreign lady who came to the orphanage and worked for free. She had friends from overseas who sent clothes and money for medical care. That's how I got my heart fixed. Caretaker Wong told me that the orphanage didn't want me to get the surgery because I would never be put up for adoption. But this foreign lady insisted. I'm fine now, but they still won't show me because of the pocks."

"What about the foreign lady? Why didn't she take you?"

I shrugged. "She had her own children. She tried to get them to show me. Said that lots of foreigners wouldn't care about the pocks. Some were even willing to take kids with medical problems. But the orphanage doesn't believe that. Besides, we don't get many foreigners. They go to the bigger institutions in Taiyuan. And there are more than enough normal babies. People mostly want the babies."

By then we had fed all the babies in the cribs against the walls and had started on the ones in the center of the room. I could see Luli looking at me, this time examining each pock. I didn't mind. I even tipped my chin up so she could get a better view. She reached over, spoon still in hand, and with her little finger she touched my face in four spots, counting, "One, two, three, four. Like the arrow."

"What?" I asked.

"The arrow in the sky. Granddad showed me in the stars at night." Her mouth trembled, and I could tell she was going to cry. I'd seen so much crying here. I tried to ignore it, but if everyone started crying, it annoyed me. She closed her eyes, trying to hold back the tears, but they seeped out and began to slide down her face.

The babies were wailing for their food. I went back to feeding them. When I looked over at Luli, her eyes were still wet. Her shoulders began to heave, and then she was sobbing. The little girl closest to her was screaming, leaning over the crib rail. She grabbed Luli's arm, and this time the bowl fell clattering to the floor, the last lumps of millet spilling out.

I ran over, thrust my bowl into her hands, and began

scraping the food back into the fallen dish. I stood up and pushed food into baby girl's mouth. The baby stopped crying and so did Luli. Her red-rimmed eyes were shocked.

"But that food was on the floor!" she said, wiping the tears from her face.

I shrugged. "Doesn't matter. They'll eat it. See?" I had put a spoonful into the next gaping mouth. "Besides, there won't be any more if we don't give it to them."

❖❖❖

The orphanage seems like another life. I glance over at the restaurant. Luli and my roommates are still eating.

"Zhenzhen and Hong will take care of her," I say to Yong.

An amused grin comes briefly to his face as he takes another shot. He says nothing else, and for a while I just watch him play.

I'm glad to see my old friend from the orphanage, and maybe I should feel bad that I left her, but I want to be with Yong.

I met Yong last month through Ming, my old boyfriend from school who helped me get a position at the factory. Ming's a year older than me and works as a floor runner at the factory; his dad supervises our unit. Ming and Yong are friends, play pool here. When Ming found out Yong was calling me, that I was meeting up with Yong without him, he got angry—told me Yong was a bride trafficker.

I didn't know what that was, but from the way he spit it out, I figured it wasn't good. When I asked Yong about it, he gave me a hard look at first, but then he said, "Bride collector." He explained that he works for a marriage broker. He picks up brides and drives them to their new husbands. There's nothing wrong about it. Ming's just jealous because I'm with Yong now.

Yong's eyes narrow to judge the distance between the balls. He checks the angles by pointing the cue stick this way and that. Slowly he moves to my side of the table and lightly bumps my shoulder with his arm to tell me to move out of the way. I smile, peering at him through my lashes like the pretty girls in television serials. As I back a few steps away from the table, he gives me an intense, lingering look. It's the kind of hungry expression that Ming gave me, but different, because a heat blooms through me as he flexes his long back over the pool stick. In the moments Yong hovers, tuning his aim, I hold my breath. Then in a quick, hard move, he sets the balls to clattering and smacking.

What I've done with Ming, I've done because he helped me. With Yong, it's going to be different. When I'm near him, my pulse speeds up and I can feel my body humming. My head feels both foggy and clear at once. Foggy when it comes to everything and everyone around me, crystal clear about what I want. Since I went out of the Institute, I've seen that I can get the things I want. And I've decided that what I want is Yong.

✦✦✦

On the back of Yong's motorbike with my arms wrapped around him, we speed through the city, the roar of the engine loud in my ears. At night, the ugly smog falls away as the lights of the city come on—lighted signs of every color overhead, streetlights and headlights in every direction. I hold tight as Yong weaves us around the cars, ignoring the blare of horns and traffic signals to keep us zipping along. When he picks up speed, my hand tightens around his chest, and I inhale the scent of him.

He drives us around awhile until we come to a dirt lane where he has a room on the backside of a rundown building.

Inside, he grabs a Coke, drops into a chair, and begins to fan himself. I glance around as I put my bag on the table. The room is half as large as my dorm, with a narrow metal bed at the back of the room, peeling green paint on the lower half of the walls, cloth tacked over the window beside the door.

I sit in the chair beside him and lean against him. He turns to me, and I lean forward for a kiss. This time the kissing doesn't end with me pulling back, like the other times he's kissed me. Instead, I let it grow more hungry and wet, and soon I'm pressing against his cheek, arms, skin. His hands and limbs wrap around me, and soon we're stroking up against each other. I only have to stretch a little in the direction of the bed and he stands me up, his body long against me, rubbing as he sway-walks me toward it.

The springs creak with our weight. The pressure of his body on top of me, wet sounds of his mouth, warm tongue, skin—all I feel is the humming of my body, calling out for more rubbing, more touching, a craving so strong. All thoughts fall away as I push down my jeans. Yong props up onto his knees and helps me yank them off. He tosses them aside and rolls beside me to shed his own pants and shirt. A moment later he's looming over me and I am caught up in his scent again. The heat of his skin, our legs entwined, all the time nuzzling and kissing as he pushes my shirt up over my head. He reaches up under the mattress and flips beside me onto his back.

"What is it?" I pant impatiently.

"Condom." He holds up a small square of plastic between two fingers.

"Oh." Ming never wore one.

As if he's reading my mind, Yong says, "A lot of guys don't like to use them, but I know better."

Yong smiles in a superior way, tears the square open, and strokes the condom onto himself.

In a second, he's back on top of me, and I'm pulling him inside me.

CHAPTER 3

Luli

I'm leaving the restaurant with Yun's roommates when Yun and her boyfriend—Yong, Zhenzhen called him—roar past on his motorbike, the smoky exhaust from the tailpipe burning the inside of my nose.

The sun has dropped away, but in the light of the noodle shop window, I see Hong and Zhenzhen flash sly smiles at each other. They throw knowing grins my way, but I can only pull my mouth to a stiff line. I watch Yun getting smaller as the motorbike zooms off down the potholed street.

I trail the girls past the low buildings and construction sites back to the dorm. The halls and bathrooms are crowded as I follow Hong and Zhenzhen to the room and through the routine of getting ready for bed. When we've all washed and changed, I slip into Yun's bunk and watch the other roommates who've come off their shift. After Hong explains who I am, the others take no notice of me. They go on chatting with each other, talking or texting on their phones, settling themselves into their bunks. The girl who didn't come out with us to eat, Dali, is still reading in her bed.

At the Institute, the girls' room was so very different. There were no photos of movie stars pasted on the walls, no stuffed animals, no clutter of purses, bags, and clothes, no bright-patterned, tumbled bedding. There were only a few of us sleeping in low cots under scratchy wool blankets. All the other girls at the Institute, except Yun, were disabled and much younger than me. I used to help them get dressed and get to the dayroom to eat before I went to school.

I can't believe that it was only this morning that I gathered together my few pieces of clothing, my comb, and Yun's letters at the Institute. I collected my identification card from a silent office worker and would have gone through the gates without anyone saying goodbye to me if I hadn't run into Caretaker Wong.

"Going out now?" she called, her voice ringing across the deserted courtyard, sounding too loud.

I nodded.

"All the young women want to work in the factory now," Caretaker Wong said. "I don't see why you would turn down a good position here." She shook her head, frowning. "You would have had security. So easy for you because you already know what to do!"

It was true I knew how to lug laundry and change diapers and prop bottles up to babies. But I had not liked it there.

She paused at the door to the main building and looked back at me. "Well, come back to visit us sometime. And if you don't like your work in the factory, maybe we'll have a position open up again."

I went through the gates then, and when they clanked behind me, they sounded different than before. I turned to see the green block lettering painted on the building: Gujiao Children's Social Welfare Institute 17. My legs were wobbly. I had been waiting so long for this day, but I hesitated, fearing the next step.

Now that I'm out, it seems strange that I'm thinking about the Institute. I suppose it's the newness of all this, and Yun not being here with me—and how different she is, with her girlish manners and her stylish hair. The first time I saw Yun she had a shaven head. Her eyes seemed to take over her face because she had no eyebrows or lashes. She told me later that the caretakers shaved her head whenever she couldn't stop plucking out her hair. She then picked out her eyebrows and lashes until they were gone too. Everything eventually grew back in, and since I've known her, she's only occasionally yanked out small patches. When I asked her why she did it, she thought for several moments before she shrugged and said it made her feel better.

I try not to be disappointed that she went off with her boyfriend. I listen for footsteps outside the door, jump every time the handle turns and one of the roommates comes in. Hong said it might be hours before she comes back. I try to stay awake, but I'm so tired.

✿✿✿

The insistent beep of an alarm wakes me the next morning. For a moment I think I'm at the Institute, but then I hear the groaning and complaining of girls around me. I sit up, searching the room, morning light streaming in the window. When my eyes adjust, I see that Yun hasn't come back.

Zhenzhen offers to show me where the human resources department is. I nod gratefully and go with her to the bathroom at the end of the hall to get ready. It's crowded with girls coming in and out of the stalls and washing at the long white-tiled sinks that line one wall and the center of the room. Wires are strung over the sinks, and faded colored underwear and bras are clipped to hangers dangling overhead. The smells of damp laundry and cleanser sting my nose. Zhenzhen and I find places next to each other at the sinks. We're bent over them, splashing our faces with cold water, when I feel a rough tap on the shoulder. I look up. Yun is there, standing between Zhenzhen and me.

Zhenzhen grabs her arm. "Where were you last night? Why didn't you answer your phone? We were worried. Thought we should tell someone!"

The smile falls off Yun's face. "You didn't, did you?"

Zhenzhen shakes her head and arches her brow. "We figured you were with your boyfriend."

Yun's smile comes back, and she squeezes her shoulders up but doesn't say anything. Her face glows, and for a moment I have that odd feeling again, as if I don't know this person.

Zhenzhen leans in. "What happened?"

Yun glances around the bathroom. The crowd is thinning, but a few girls standing around us have stopped what they're doing and are plainly listening. She shakes off the question. "I have to change and get ready for work. Besides, I want to see if I can help Luli get a place."

"I was going early to take her to the Human Resources Department. Better hurry."

Yun nods. "Okay. Maybe it would be better if you introduced her, since I didn't do overtime yesterday. Remind them that there're some openings in my department. Take her to see Ming." She turns to me. "You remember Ming from school."

I do remember Ming. He was a couple years ahead of us and took notice of Yun shortly before he finished middle school. He used to trail her as we walked home. At first she was puzzled by it. She stopped on the sidewalk and shouted at him, "Why are you walking with us?" He shrugged and blushed, but just a few weeks later, they were kissing in the alley.

They were still together when Yun went out of the orphanage, but she didn't mention him in her last letter. I guess they've broken up since she's with Yong now.

Zhenzhen takes me to the canteen, and we wait outside, hoping to catch Ming on his way out. I ate so much last night that I can still feel the food in my stomach, but the smell of fry oil coming through the door as people go in and out makes my stomach rumble. I could eat again, but Zhenzhen makes no mention of it, and I don't ask.

When she spots Ming, she calls him over. He looks much the same as when I last saw him two years ago—thin, wearing a collared shirt, only now his short hair is cut so that long bangs hang in his face. He's grown taller, but he slumps with his head and shoulders forward as if he's uncomfortable with his height. As he approaches, I feel his eyes taking me in, though he doesn't seem to recognize me. I wonder if I've changed so much.

"This is Cao Luli," Zhenzhen says. "She's looking for a position. She's a friend of Yun's. Comes from that same orphanage. Yun thought you might be able to help her find something. Says there are openings in your department."

Ming cocks his head when Zhenzhen mentions Yun, and he looks at me more closely, studying my face.

"Where's Yun? Why didn't she ask me herself?"

"She's dragging behind this morning," Zhenzhen answers. "You know she was sick yesterday—couldn't do that overtime your department wanted."

His mouth twists and he shakes his head. Then he turns to me. "I remember you from school."

"Can you ask your dad, then?" Zhenzhen says. "I have to get on my line now."

He nods.

Zhenzhen leaves for her building, and I follow Ming, the moths creeping back into my stomach.

CHAPTER 4

Luli

I'm surprised at how quickly I fall into the routine of my new life. At first the days are endless. My fingertips are raw from twisting the plastic-coated wires around the USB cords, then slipping them into tiny plastic bags. As I work down my supply boxes and watch my "finished" bin fill up with neat rows of the wound cords, a bubble of satisfaction grows in my chest. But before I come to the last layer, the rolling cart arrives at my work-station and more supplies are plopped in front of me. When I look over at Yun, I wonder how she has endured working here for more than a year. Her face is vacant, eyes dull, the same as when she was feeding the babies or mopping floors at the Institute.

I soon learn to stop monitoring how close I am to emptying or filling a bin. Eventually the sting leaves my fingertips, and the skin there becomes tough and callused. I learn to wash my mind of thoughts as if I'm nothing more than a pair of hands. My neck and back are harder to ignore. They ache from hunching over the worktable, and no matter how many times I straighten up or stretch, the stiffness and knots are always there.

Though only three months have passed, I feel like I've been working forever. Each night, all I want to do is to fall into bed as soon as I can. My roommates, at least the younger ones, often go out to shop, to eat, even to dance at clubs. I've gone with them or with Yun a couple of times, but I've always felt out of place and hesitant to spend my pay. Yun once asked me what I was saving for. I couldn't think of an answer, except to say that I had never had any money. But later, I thought of how Granddad sold the goats one by one and still ran out of money for medicine.

I don't see Yun much. I've been assigned to a different dormitory building, and at work we're not allowed to talk. After work, she usually flies out of the factory and rushes off to see Yong, so I see her only during the busy lunch period as we're corralled through the canteen line, shouting over the racket of a thousand conversations and the banging of trays.

The canteen is less chaotic in the mornings. The rows of white tables and blue plastic chairs are only half filled with tired workers. Lots of the younger ones have been out late into the night and choose to sleep in rather than dragging themselves to breakfast. This morning I stand in the food-serving line with Ming. He picks up a tray from a pile as high as my shoulder and clatters it onto the metal counter. I ran into him at breakfast the first day I started work, and we've fallen into the habit of eating together. He's nice to me, and of course I'm grateful that he helped me get this job.

Some of the girls have seen us and teased me about being his girlfriend. My face always gets hot whenever they bring it up, and I always tell them we aren't together. Though part of me does wonder what that would be like.

Now, Ming tosses his head so his long bangs fling back. He points at a steaming pan of rice porridge, and the server scoops some into a bowl and hands it to him. As we step forward in the line, he says, "Yun's boyfriend is a kidnapper."

I'm not sure I heard right over the shouts of the cooks and servers. "Kidnapper?"

"Yes. You should tell her to stay away from him." I can't see his expression. His back is to me as he pushes his tray forward, pointing at the pans. The kitchen workers lump food onto each segment of his divided plastic tray.

"Why are you kidding like that?" I ask, feeling a prick of jealousy that he's thinking about Yun.

"Not kidding." He glances back at me, shakes his head. "He is a kidnapper. Or he helps one. They kidnap girls and women and sell them to men out in the countryside." He could be telling me that Yun is going to work overtime for all the casualness in his voice. Or pretend casualness.

I frown, not believing him. "Yun said he was a bride collector."

Ming makes a face. "All the women have left the countryside to work in the cities and big towns. The men pay for the girls, then marry them."

"But Yong doesn't kidnap them! Yun says he just picks up the brides. Drives them to their new home, like a car service." There's a tightening in my chest, a feeling of disquiet. I'm not sure if it's for Yun or for myself. I try to get a look at Ming's face to see if he really thinks this is true.

"I guess I thought that too when I first met him. But now I know. Some of the guys we both know explained it to me. Yong just uses that as his cover, because who can say, 'Hello there, I kidnap people and sell them'?'"

I try to make sense of what Ming is telling me as we reach the end of the line and pay for our food. I shake my head. "Can't be. They've been spending all their time together for months now. If he was going to kidnap Yun, he would have done it already."

"Maybe he's not planning to kidnap *her*. Maybe he really

likes her. Doesn't mean he hasn't trafficked other girls." He shrugs and heads to an empty table near the window.

I follow him and plunk down my tray with a touch of annoyance. I think of that day I saw Ming kissing Yun in the alley, rubbing his hands all over her. He was with Yun for a long time, the girls have told me. Right up until she met Yong. I wonder if he still wants her.

"Even if he's not going to sell her," Ming says, steadily scooping food into his mouth, "a guy like that is bad."

A guy like that is bad, but I don't say anything. Jealousy is keeping me quiet.

"I thought you didn't care about her anymore," I say.

"I don't." He glances up, indignation in his voice. "Not like that." He shrugs again and sweeps his bangs aside. "But she's your friend. You should worry about her, shouldn't you?"

I swirl the thick rice porridge on my tray. Cold now. I'm not sure I believe what he says. And I don't think Yun would listen to me anyway, because she's crazy about Yong. But it's true that she's my friend.

᭡ ᭡ ᭡

At work, I glance toward the door, across the rows and rows of long tables with heads bowed over them. Rows of fluorescent lamps hang overhead, directly above the tables. One has a bad bulb, and every now and again, it flashes and disturbs the even white light of the room. The other workers don't seem to notice. They're all doing their tasks, already settled in their own thoughts.

I worry about Yun. She's late. Already so late that I wonder if she's going to make it or lose another day. In the few months

I've worked here, she's been late several times, sometimes just a few minutes, sometimes more. She's suffered docks to her pay and awful lectures from Foreman Chen. I don't know how many more times she can get away with it.

Suddenly she's at the door, pulling on her work jacket. I steal a look at Foreman Chen, who is stalking the aisles with his arms crossed. He lowers his heavy black glasses to peer at someone's work in the row in front of mine. Yun starts to clock in, but he spots her before she can swipe her badge.

"Stop right there!" Foreman Chen shouts across the work floor. His voice booms over the whir of the air-handling system. Workers' heads startle up and their hands freeze for just a second before they go back to work, while their eyes flick between their cords and Foreman Chen and Yun.

"Don't do it!" Foreman Chen raises an angry finger at her and storms over toward the time clock. His thick middle strains against the tuck of his shirt in his waistband as he moves. "Don't swipe!"

Yun drops the badge, letting it dangle from the lanyard around her neck, and turns to face Foreman Chen. Her face is pale and sulky. I will her to look a little more sorry.

"You're late again!" Foreman Chen stands before her with his hands on his hips, not bothering to lower his voice. "How many times does that make this quarter? This is not how a responsible worker behaves."

The overhead light shines on his bare scalp where the long thin hair he has combed over has slipped away. He doesn't seem to notice the strands brushing against his cheek. "And how much sick time have you taken in the last quarter? Once you took a full day. Another day you couldn't stay for the overtime!"

Yun's gaze has gone to the floor. I can't tell if she's ashamed or if she doesn't care. Again, I will her to apologize, plead, cry. Anything to keep her job. But she only stands with her head bent. She mumbles something I can't hear.

"Sick? Sick again?" Foreman Chen draws back his neck, then flings his hands out. "But you're here. If you're well enough now, why couldn't you be here forty minutes ago?"

She looks up at him now. The unblemished side of her face is turned to the workroom, and I notice how thin she has become. She seems tired, but from this side, with her shagged hair behind her ear, anyone would think she's a perfect beauty. All at once her expression changes, and I know she's decided to try. I still can't hear what she's saying, but I can see that a rush of words spills from her mouth. She makes her eyes sad, and when she isn't turning them toward Foreman Chen, she dips her head down like a beaten dog.

Yun is using her acting skills. I remember when she started practicing, a few years after I came to the orphanage. We were shuttling the two- and three-year-olds to the toilet chairs and their baths. The TV was on, playing a soap opera the caretakers liked to watch. The kids were propped in the wooden seats that kept them from crawling or walking around. They chewed on their fingers and stared at the television. I untied the bindings of one little girl who couldn't sit up on her own and carried her to the bathroom at the back of the dayroom.

One of the caretakers scrubbed a little girl at the big sink, while Yun squatted to undress a boy who had a paralyzed arm. She twisted around awkwardly so she could watch the television through the doorway.

"Help me," I said to Yun, holding up my girl. Yun shifted so her eyes could stay glued to the television, then yanked down the girl's pants. I plopped her onto one of the potties and held her up while Yun tied her to the seat. She finished undressing her boy, passed him to the caretaker, and started drying off the girl who had just been bathed. I started wiping another girl sitting on a third pot when I noticed Yun, still staring at the television, making faces. She tilted her head and fluttered her eyelids, a fake smile on her face. Then she bobbled her head like she was laughing and opened her mouth, though no noise came out.

I had my girl undressed, switched her out with the boy who had just been washed, and crouched next to Yun to dry him. "What are you doing?"

"Practicing my emotions." She didn't take her eyes off the screen as she dressed the child.

"What do you mean?"

"When that group toured the other day, I heard one of the interpreters tell the director that the foreigner was disturbed that the children seemed sad and unemotional."

I glanced toward the children stuck in their seats. Most of them were just sitting, staring at nothing. Almost all of them had mental or physical problems. They hardly ever laughed or cried.

"The lively ones always get the most attention. They don't stay here long. I'm practicing so I'll get picked when I'm shown."

That alarmed me. Yun was my only friend here. There were others, like Guo, but they didn't talk much. "Have they put through your documentation?"

"No." She hung her head and made a long face. She tried to act sad, but her eyes moved back and forth, not sad at all. I suppressed the urge to laugh.

Yun never did get shown. But whenever the television was on, she studied the faces of the actors and copied their movements.

Now, Foreman Chen crosses his arms, squinting at Yun as she talks. I can tell he's pleased that she is making an appropriate plea in front of the other workers. He lets her talk until she wipes the corner of her eye with a knuckle.

"This is not acceptable." Foreman Chen shakes his head slowly. He finally notices his out-of-place strands of hair and rakes them back. "We must have workers who are reliable. Even though you were an orphan, I gave you a chance. In fact, you might say I've given you many chances, all the times I overlooked your lateness. Most places wouldn't take a risk on someone like you. Besides those who are superstitious about orphans, the more practical ones think if you don't have a family, you don't know how to take responsibility for others. Won't be dependable."

Yun drops her hand from the tears I can't quite see. Her mouth turns small. The muscles of her jaw tighten.

"When I hired you, you promised me that you would work extra hard to make up for being an orphan. Plenty of people would like a place here. So many girls are willing to work hard, work when they're sick, eager for the overtime so they can make extra money for their families. I hope you'll think about that in your next position. You've run out of chances here. You're fired." He holds his hand out for her badge.

Yun's mouth drops open in shock. She stands there for what seems like a long time. I've stopped working to watch, holding my breath. I really don't know what she's going to do.

She whips her badge over her head and throws it at Foreman Chen. It hits him in the chest, and he grapples to catch it, but it falls to the floor. Yun spins around and runs out the door as Foreman Chen bends to pick up the badge. When he straightens up, he pats back his hair and scans the room. We all go back to work, pretending we haven't been watching.

Ming is standing at the end of my row with his pushcart. He throws me a glance before Foreman Chen, his father, ticks his head for him to get back to work.

Yun's been fired. Where will she go? What will happen now? I know everyone says it's easy to get jobs. I've seen several girls go to new positions. Hong moved to another factory a few weeks ago. But is it as easy if you've been fired from your last position? And where will Yun live while she looks for something else?

All morning I watch the clock ticking toward the lunch hour. When the bell finally rings, I throw on my cheap polyester coat while I push with the others out of the building. I'll go to Yun's room. Maybe I can catch her while she's still packing up.

But as soon as I'm out the main door, I hear someone shouting my name. It takes a moment for my eyes to adjust to the smog-white sky. But at last I spot Yun pushing toward me against the people flooding out the door. She grabs my arm, and we find a concrete bench in the factory plaza. I can feel the coldness of it through my pants and cheap new coat.

"Yun, what are you going to do now? Do you think you can find another position?" I'm thinking of Foreman Chen's words. And of what the caretakers always said: *No one wants to hire orphans.*

"I don't know! I can't think about that right now." She tosses her head irritably. "I need you to come with me."

"What do you mean? Where?"

She huffs out a breath and slumps, then puts her hands up to her face, patting at her own cheeks. "Will you go with me to the health clinic?"

"Why? What's the matter?"

She doesn't answer at first, just drops her hands and stares out. People are standing and moving in all directions on the plaza, but she isn't looking at anything in particular. "I have to get a pregnancy test."

My hand flies to my mouth. I'm too shocked to say anything. My mind jams, trying to grasp what this means. All those sly comments that the other girls make. I suddenly feel so dumb for not realizing it. Yun has been having sex with Yong. That first night I slept in her bunk, she didn't come home. I got my own room assignment that next day, so I've had no idea of her comings and goings.

Yun starts crying. She isn't acting now. The best I can do is pat her arm.

"You'll come with me? After your shift. They're open late. I don't want to go by myself."

"What about Yong?"

She swipes at the tears streaming down her face. "I don't want to tell him until I know for sure. Anyway, he's out of town. Working on a job."

On a job. *Bride collecting?*

CHAPTER 5

Yun

The TV blares overhead with a costume drama. The other four women in the waiting room of the Modern Women's Health Clinic sit with their arms crossed over their bags or coats, some leaning against their boyfriends or husbands, all gazing up at the screen. I slump in my chair, plucking hairs from the nape of my neck while I wait for the clerk to call me back in again. We waited for almost two hours before I first got called back for a short talk with a doctor, and now almost another hour has passed while I wait for my test. In that time, I've picked out nearly a bird's nest of hair even though I've been trying not to.

It helps that Luli is here beside me, sitting on the edge of her hard seat. Her face is shadowed by the floor lamp beside her chair. Her worried eyes keep shifting to me. I know she has questions, but I can't talk now, so I stare out the streaked window with only the furtive little pinches at my neck to calm me.

The sky is purply-dark outside. Across the street, the street-light with the tilting pole shines down on the pool tables where I first met Yong. There are only a few guys shooting—laborers, judging by the look of their military surplus coats marked with the white dust of construction sites. I can see that the wind has picked up from the way they pull the coats around them as they wait for their shot, how they hunch nearly doubled over to light their cigarettes.

The clinic door opens, and a middle-aged woman comes through, bringing in a draft of cold air and the smell of frying meat from the restaurant next door. I feel my stomach rumble. I haven't had anything to eat all day except a few bites of rice, which Luli smuggled out of the dining hall for me at lunchtime. I said I was too sick to eat it and would just throw it up, but she wouldn't go back to work until she saw me eat something. I didn't throw it up, but now I'm really hungry. The custodian from the bathroom this morning was right when she said my appetite would come by evening.

I felt so sick when I woke up today that I just wanted to stay curled up in my bunk. But when my stomach started talking to me, I dragged myself out of bed and ran to the bathroom. It was empty by then because everyone had already gone to work. I flung myself into a stall. The smell coming from the squat toilet was all it took to bring up everything I had eaten yesterday. I stooped over, retching and retching until I felt like my insides had come out. When I straightened up, I was dizzy and had to lean against the partition before I could make my way out of the stall.

The custodian stood just inside the bathroom door. Her gray-streaked hair was pulled back in a loose bun, and her hand was planted on her hip. The other hand held a mop in a rolling bucket. She glared at me suspiciously. "What's going on?"

"Nothing. I was sick."

She squinted at my middle. "Are you pregnant?"

"No!" I stepped to the sink and started washing out my mouth and splashing my face.

She pushed her bucket to the far end of the bathroom and

began swabbing the mop against the floor. "Maybe you are, and you just don't know it. You have a boyfriend?"

I ignored her. I didn't have my towel, so I tried to pat my face dry as best as I could with my hands. In the mirror, my face was white, almost greenish under the fluorescent light and opaque glass window. I looked like a ghost.

"I know how it is with you young girls. You don't know anything. I've been working here seven years now. I've seen this happen lots of times."

She lifted the mop and dashed it in the bucket water several times. "And I've been pregnant myself," she declared proudly before she bent over to twist out the mop with her raw, red hands. "Oh, I was so sick. Not just in the morning, but sick all day. For months. Didn't know what was wrong with me. Seemed like I was wasting away. The only time I could eat anything was at night when I started to feel better. I would get so hungry, but I hated to eat too much because the next morning I would be throwing it all up."

She smiled to herself, like all that was a happy memory, all the time sloshing her mop back and forth, while I felt my stomach tightening with panic.

"I was married though." Her eyebrows arched a warning. "You better get a test. Don't wait too long. The abortion's easier if you do it early."

Now, at the clinic, that same panic comes back to me. The office worker behind the glass window shouts out my name. Luli and I rise and go back again, but instead of pointing to the office where I told the doctor my symptoms earlier, the clerk gestures to another room along the hall. We head that way.

In the tiny, windowless room, I see an examination table and a large piece of equipment on wheels with corded instruments hooked on the side and a computer screen on top. A woman wearing a pink smock waves us in. "Who's getting the sonogram?"

I step forward, and she gestures for me to lie down.

"Pull up your shirt and push down your pants a little." She squirts a blue gel on an instrument attached to the computer by a cord and puts it against my stomach. I'm startled by the coldness of the gel, but she quickly starts rubbing it around, pushing and prodding. Her eyes are glued to the screen, which I can't see from where I lie. Luli stands near the closed door, looking scared, her eyes flicking between my belly and the screen. She's watching the screen when her mouth falls open.

"What is it?" I raise up on my elbow.

Before Luli has a chance to answer, the technician taps a few keys on the computer and hands me some paper towels. "You're done. Take this back to the office. They'll give you the results." She hands me a printout, two mostly black images I hardly have a chance to glimpse as I wipe my stomach and climb off the table.

In the hallway, Luli huddles next to me and we examine the blurry picture. The misshapen bean-like image is unmistakable. It is definitely a baby.

Luli covers her mouth with her hand and grips my arm. Her eyes shine excitedly.

I can't believe that there's something growing inside me. I can't feel more empty. A hungry stomach, the weeks of queasiness, being humiliated and losing my job, and now this. A baby. What will Yong say about it?

"What are we going to do?" Luli asks.

She said *we*, but *I* have no idea.

Luli tugs on my jacket. "Well, let's go talk to the doctor."

We go to the office where two doctors sit at desks with their computers. We wait our turn for the one we saw earlier, who gave me the slip to pay for the sonogram. She waves us over. I sit in the metal chair beside her desk and hand her the images.

She glances at them. "You're pregnant. Married?"

I shake my head.

"It's a termination then?" It's less a question than a statement, and she starts to jot on a form.

I look at Luli. Her stupefied expression is no help to me. I shrug.

The doctor catches the look and stops writing. "Unless you can pay the social compensation fee for having an unauthorized pregnancy, you won't be able to get a birth permit." I'm still staring at her blankly, so she goes on: "Without a permit you can't give birth at a hospital. If you give birth at home, you'll still be fined. And you'll have to pay off those fines in order to get the child's hukou." The hukou is the government registration that makes you an official person. I needed mine to get hired at the factory.

The doctor studies me for a moment, not smiling, not exactly frowning. "So I assume you'll want to terminate?"

When I don't say anything, she begins pecking at her computer. "Next, you have to have a few more tests. Go back to the clerk and pay for the ECG to check your heart. Hand over this slip when they call you for it. After that you'll have to come back in here with the results. Then I'll give you the payslip for a blood test. And there will also be an internal exam. If everything is good, you'll choose whether you want the medical abortion or the surgical procedure. The medical procedure costs 450 yuan. You'll take two pills to terminate and expel the fetus under medical supervision. There will be cramping and bleeding, and you may continue to have some spotting for a few weeks afterward, but you can return to work in just a few days. The alternative is vacuum suction under anesthesia and—"

"Wait!" Luli blurts out. "Is the baby a boy or a girl?"

The doctor makes an irritated noise. "It's illegal for us to reveal the sex." The contempt in the doctor's expression is impossible to miss. "You think it will make a difference to your boyfriend? He's not even here with you."

"He's on a work trip!" I glare back at her. "I started wondering this morning and didn't even wait for him to get home before I decided to come down here!" I don't know why I feel the need to explain. I don't like the way she speaks, I don't like the chain of tests, I don't want to be here.

I stand up, just wanting to get out. "I should talk to him before I decide anything." I turn to Luli. "Let's get out of here!"

Outside the clinic, the blast of cold wind driving sand and bits of construction debris against my cheeks feels good. I didn't realize how stifling it was in there.

Luli holds her arm over her face, cowering against the wind. I lead her to the restaurant next door and find seats for us in the corner, away from the other people eating, chatting, laughing with no worries. We order, and then Luli can't stay quiet anymore.

"Yun." Her eyes are wide. "What do you think Yong will want to do?"

I pluck a chopstick out of its holding glass and tap it nervously against the table. I really don't know what he'll say.

I try to play out the scene in my mind. Will I tell him right away? Or will I wait to whisper it in his ear while we're in bed?

Luli doesn't wait for me to answer before she's leaning in

with her anxious expression. "You'll get married, right? You've been together all this time. If you get married, you won't have to worry about getting another position."

I stare at her. Marriage? I'm not even legal age yet.

"You can stay home and take care of the baby."

I see myself in Yong's room with a squalling infant. Feeding, washing, the smell of dirty diapers. The Institute rushes at me. In my mind I see the rows of crying infants in their cribs at the orphanage. Sometimes when the crying escalated, I just wanted to knock my head against the wall or pull my hair out or run out of the building.

Luli persists. "You already know what to do. You know all about how to take care of babies."

I wince and pull a face. I may know how to take care of babies, but I didn't like it much. I certainly don't know how to be a mother. "Yong goes away to work, and I'd be by myself for days at a time. Taking care of a baby alone! That was so stupid of me to run out of the clinic. I'll have to go back."

Luli's eyes widen with horror. I don't know why she thinks this is such a big deal.

"I'll need to borrow the money from Yong," I press on. "But I'm sure that won't be a problem."

The woman brings the food. I devour it like a starved rat. Several minutes pass before I notice that Luli isn't eating. She's inspecting her hands when she's not throwing me anxious glances. "Aren't you hungry?" I ask.

She doesn't answer for a while longer. Finally, she asks quietly, "Do you . . . trust Yong?"

I wrinkle my forehead in confusion. "Trust him? You just asked me if I was going to *marry* him."

"Yes, well, I thought . . ." She shrugs, embarrassed. "I guess

I thought if you got married, that would be one thing. He'd have to support you then. He wouldn't be able to . . ."

"To what?"

Luli leans forward and says in a low voice, "Yun, Ming says Yong is a bride trafficker."

This again. I frown. "What are you talking about? I told you he drives women to their new husbands. *Escorts* them, he says."

"Are you sure?" She pulls back her lip in that timid way. "Ming says that men in the countryside pay Yong's boss to locate girls for them. They trick or kidnap them and then sell them."

"Not true!" I can't believe Luli is saying this. Or that Ming would feed her such a story. "A horrible lie. Ming! You know he's just mad at Yong and me. Jealous that we started up!"

"Shhh." Luli glances around. People are staring at us. "I don't think he's jealous." She blinks a few times. "Not anymore, anyway. He knows we're friends, and he . . . he just thought I should tell you."

Thoughts crash around in my brain. I know it isn't true. Luli is stupid to believe this story. She can't see what Ming is doing. Yong . . . he wouldn't. I shake my head at Luli. "Well, if he's a bride trafficker, why hasn't he sold me? All these months, he could've kidnapped me anytime he felt like it, if that was what he wanted."

"I'm sure he really likes you," Luli says hastily. "But—what if he gets angry when he finds out about the baby? What if he decides he wants to be done with you? If he has a choice between giving you money for the termination and *making* money by selling you—"

I don't have to listen to this poison. "Not true. Not true!" I throw down my chopsticks, grab my coat, and run out of there without even finishing my food.

CHAPTER 6

Yun

I run from the restaurant into the poorly lit street. I'm out
of breath by the time I burst onto Xifu Road. I stop and lean
against a bicycle rack, lightheaded. Silver specks float in my
vision. Everything is spinning. People and cars crossing every
direction. Bright store signs and traffic lights flashing. Honking from the four lanes hammering my ears. I close my eyes
and take a few gulps of the biting air before my head is straight
enough for me to get moving again.

The temperature is dropping, and the cold stings my
cheeks. I don't know where I'm going. I just start walking,
dodging people chaining up their bicycles, people rushing by
or waiting for the buses—probably going home to their families. The lights from the dingy small shops spill out onto the
sidewalks. Through their glass doors, I can see the owners
standing and eating their dinners, watching the street.

I walk several blocks before I get the idea to go to Yong's
place. I realize I'm headed that direction anyway. I don't know
if he'll be home. The last time I saw him was when we went to
the night market two nights ago. He didn't say when he was
coming home.

Bride trafficker.

I shake my head, my anger rising again. Luli doesn't know what she's talking about. Yong is a driver. He works for a marriage broker.

We actually ran into his boss at the night market the other evening when we went to get some snacks. It wasn't as cold then, and the market was crowded. We ate skewered meat and fried bread while we wandered among the tented stalls, under the stringed lights and flagged banners that crisscrossed over the lane. My eyes ran over the tables and racks loaded with belts, watches, electronics, plastic toys. I pointed at things I wanted to buy with my next pay, but each time I had to nudge Yong because his face was always bored-looking or pointed the other way, scanning the faces in the crowd. He hadn't wanted to go out, but I had whined until he agreed. When I saw the stall with athletic shoes I thought he would like, I tugged on his hand and pulled him toward them.

"Wait a minute." Yong craned his head around the crowd as if he'd spotted someone he knew. He dropped my hand. "Stay here. I'll be right back." Skirting the crowd, he walked over to a man at least ten years older than him. They talked several minutes before Yong came back to me.

"Who was that?" I asked.

"My boss." Yong moved us back toward the shoes.

I glanced back for another look, but he had disappeared in the crowd.

"What did he want?"

"He just needs me to drive somewhere tomorrow."

"Where?"

"Don't ask so many questions."

I don't know why, but that grated on me. "You're taking somebody to her new husband? Where are you picking her up?"

He shrugged and began to pick up shoes, studying each pair. He never talked about his work. He just went away, usually unexpectedly, and stayed for however long and came back when he came back. I wouldn't hear from him for days at a time. "I don't know," he finally said.

"Your boss didn't even tell you where you're supposed to go?"

Yong sighed impatiently and gave me an awful look.

I hated that cold feeling he gave me, like I was some stranger. The rush of early times when we first met, when he had looked at me with smiles and adoring eyes, felt so far away. Lately when I saw him, he was often distant and didn't even hold my hand. When we went back to his room, we would have sex, and then he would smoke, watch TV, roll off to sleep. At first I didn't mind too much, but I had begun to feel bored myself. Still, I didn't like to see him cross with me, so I plucked up a pair of sneakers and danced them on top of the other shoes, singing, "But you make so much nice money."

He smirked then, and the night had gone on like always.

But now . . . I stop on the sidewalk, press my clenched hands against my stomach. I should have gone ahead and scheduled the termination, but I just had to get out of that place.

I'm in Yong's neighborhood now. The two-lane streets are quieter here, with fewer streetlights. I turn into Yong's lane. It's dark, with only faint light from a few of the neighbors' curtained windows. No stars are visible overheard, though the nighttime smog glows an unnatural yellow-gray from the illumination of the city.

At Yong's flat, the windows are dark. I knock on the door just in case he's asleep. No answer. I bang harder, even though I know that he isn't there. I don't know if he's still away on the job, or if he's back in town and just out for the night.

I sink down onto the narrow doorsill and huddle up against it while I think about what to do next. If Yong doesn't come home tonight, I don't know where I'll stay. Gatekeeper Wu at the factory let me stash my things under the desk in the gate-house, but I'll have to pick them up soon.

I pull my wallet out of my bag and try to count my money, holding the bills toward the neighbor's window to make them out. After the cost of the sonogram, I only have 532 yuan. And I'll need that just to get by until I find another position.

I know I should have saved more. Some girls, like Luli and Dali, my roommate, never spend any money. Always eating at the canteen, never buying new clothes or going to the dance clubs. Dali sends most of her pay home to her family.

My only hope is that Yong will give me the money for the termination.

I stuff the money back into my wallet, push it deep inside my bag, plunk my head back against the door, and begin pulling out strands of hair. I wonder about the woman who left me on the side of the road. I can't call her my mother. So many times over the years I've wondered about her, but I never get far in my imagining. She didn't leave a sad, pleading note tucked inside my blankets like some of the mothers who abandoned their babies did. The caretakers supposed she left me near the entrance to the supermarket because of my pocks and my bad heart, because she couldn't afford to have it fixed, or because she wasn't married, or because she was married and they wanted to have a boy. It could have been any reason.

Someone turns into the alley, a dark silhouette against the light of the nearby street. I stand and step up onto the low door-sill, pull my coat tightly around myself, and squint, trying to make out if it's Yong.

After a moment, I can see that it isn't him. This person is thick around the middle and wears a long coat that flaps around his legs. I slump back against the door, disappointed. It's really getting cold. I ran from Luli before I finished eating, and now I still feel hungry. If I go to get something to eat, I can also sit inside a warm restaurant. I just don't want to miss Yong.

The man stops in front of me. "Is this Number 8, Wuyi Lane?" he asks. He wears a flat wool cap that shadows his broad face from the light of the neighbor's window, but I can see frameless rectangular glasses perching on his wide nose.

"Yes."

"I'm looking for Liang Yong."

"He's not here."

"But this is his residence?"

I nod.

"Who are you?"

"I'm . . . a friend. I'm waiting for him too."

"Is he coming home soon?"

I shrug. "Don't know. He may be working."

He studies me. I wonder who he is. He's too old to be one of Yong's friends—even older than Yong's boss. With his cap and long coat, he looks like one of the officials who occasionally inspected the orphanage. I start to feel nervous, as if I'm about to be scolded by Foreman Chen at the factory.

"You're a friend? Would you say, girlfriend?"

I shrug again. It's none of his business.

"I'm a detective. Hired by a family to find their daughter." He hands me a business card, which I can't read because of the darkness. "Did you know that Liang Yong is a bride trafficker?"

My breath catches in my chest. I'm frozen in place, yet my

head suddenly becomes very hot. The light from the neighbors' windows refracts in the detective's glasses as he takes a step forward.

"Where has he gone?"

I can't say anything. I only shake my head slightly.

"I've given you a shock." His voice softens. "You'd better get away from him. You're in real danger. These bride traffickers sometimes get girls by wooing them. They find girls on dating websites, on chat rooms. The man will act like a boyfriend. He'll tell a girl they're going to go on a weekend trip together, take the girl far away from home, then sell her to a man in the countryside."

I pinch my lips together, trembling. Maybe Ming put him up to this.

"How long have you been going around with Liang Yong?"

I don't want to answer him, but his eyes stay fixed on me until I drop my hand and mumble, "Three months."

His face twitches. I have the feeling he's surprised.

"Yes!" I snap. "Really, more than three months! See, you're wrong about Yong! It's not him!" I'm about to tell him that it's Yong's boss he must be looking for, but I realize that I should keep my mouth shut.

The detective shakes his head. "I don't know why he's kept you for so long," he murmurs. "Using you for himself? Maybe his customers aren't so choosy about that. But I'm telling you, this man is a dangerous person. He kidnaps people! Young women like you. Can you imagine being taken away from your family and forced to submit to a strange man? You'd have to clean his house, cook his food, have his baby. For the rest of your life, you'd be trapped. This is going to happen to you if you let yourself be tricked."

My face burns. Why do older people feel like they can say anything and tell you what to do? Even the girls from the factory with their prodding questions don't talk to me like this. This man is even worse than the doctor at the clinic. I don't have to believe him.

He speaks gently again. "Get away from him before it's too late. Go home."

Go home. If he only knew Yong's home is the only one I have.

Still, I step off the doorsill and duck past him and head toward the street. I just want to get away.

"If you see him, don't tell him that I'm looking for him," he calls out to me.

I don't turn around. I stuff his card deep into my pocket.

CHAPTER 7

Luli

After Yun storms out of the restaurant, I hastily pay for the food, but by the time I get out to the street, she's nowhere in sight. I rush back to the factory. I try her old room, thinking her roommates might've sneaked her in and let her stay overnight. Her things are gone, and the other girls haven't seen her. We try calling her from their mobiles, but she doesn't answer. Yun's always chiding me because I still don't have a phone. "Who would want to call me?" I say. She always answers that she would, that it would be easier for us to keep in touch, but I still haven't gotten one. I finally go to bed, wishing I'd listened to her.

At breakfast, I tell Ming about my fight with Yun—leaving out the part about the baby, of course. Nobody talks about that kind of thing. "I need to find her," I say to him. "Can you think of anywhere she might be?"

Ming doesn't meet my eyes. "She's probably just angry that my dad fired her. Don't worry. I'm sure you'll hear from her once she's calmed down."

I shake my head. I can't just leave it at that. I have to make sure she's all right. And I have to apologize for what I said to her. I shouldn't have repeated a rumor, stuck my nose in something

I know nothing about. She had a good point, after all—if Yong is really dangerous, wouldn't he have shown it by now? Anyway, I hate that she's mad at me. "Please, Ming," I say. "I just have to know that she's safe."

He sighs. "You could try looking for her at Cradle Club tonight." The name's familiar. I went there once before with Yun and her roommates. I hadn't liked the pulsing lights and the loud music thumping in my ears, and when the girls dragged me out to the crowded dance floor, I had felt stiff and mechanical. I flinch, thinking about going back there. "I'm not sure I remember the way," I say hesitantly, and Ming sighs again.

"I'll go with you."

♣ ♣ ♣

After dinner, Ming and I head out to look for Yun. Though it's full dark, the factory entrance is bright as day, lit by the plaza's floodlights. The gatekeeper with the thin moustache pulls it open for us as we approach. When he gets a good look at me, recognition comes over his face.

"Hey!" he barks at us. "Tell your friend she needs to get her stuff!" He steps over to the guardbox, flings the door open, and points at three large plastic bags shoved into a corner. Yun's bright pink comforter overflows from one of the bags. "She should have gotten it last night." He glares at me like this was my fault. "I told the other guard that I'll throw it out at the end of my shift if she doesn't pick it up by then. That's in a few hours! I don't mind doing her a favor, but I won't get in trouble for it."

I look at Ming, who only raises his brows. I nod to the guard, and as we hurry through, what he told me begins to

54

sink in. I wonder if Ming feels the same worry—that Yun has been without her things since last night—but his face shows nothing. I speed up to keep pace with him as he leads me through the streets.

At the club, we have no trouble getting past the bouncer, even though I'm sure I don't look eighteen. I've quickly learned that most places like this don't enforce the drinking age. Although it's pretty early in the night, several people are already standing at the high tables with their drinks, the women swaying on their heels, the guys smoking and leaning on their elbows. I scan the faces, searching for Yun. Colored dots of light swirl around the dark room. Bright strobes flash like lightning and make everyone on the dance floor look like they're seizing. I feel dizzy myself. The *wup-wupping* music and flashing lights make me feel strange, disoriented. Though I've been here before, I feel deeply that I don't know this place.

Ming grabs my elbow and quickly leads me on a circuit through the club. The music thunders in my ears. When Ming says something to me, I can't hear him.

"What?" I shout.

He leans in and cups his mouth near my ear. "She's not here! Let's go."

"Where?"

Ming shrugs.

I sigh. We just got here and rushed through the club. I do want to leave, but I'm not ready to give up. "Maybe we missed her. Let's go around again!" I shout. I don't know what else to do.

Impatience creeps into his face. "It's no use. She isn't here."

"Well, we came all this way. It won't hurt to go around one more time."

Ming rolls his eyes, but we thread our way through, more slowly this time, glancing between the dancers and the people clumped up at the tables. I don't see her. We end up back at the black-painted entry alcove, where the noise isn't so deafening, though cold air blasts in each time the door opens.

"Okay?" Ming thumbs toward the door. "Let's get out of here."

I have to agree. "Where should we try next?"

"Don't know." He casts his eyes around the room distractedly. "I think we should go back. I'm tired. I want to go home."

I'm tired too, thanks to sleeping badly, then working a full shift, all the time worrying about Yun. But if I go back to the dorm, I know I'll sit up worrying again. I don't like that she got so angry with me, but she's like that. I know she'll get over it if only I can talk to her. I only want to help her. She's pregnant, fired, with only a possible bride trafficker to rely on. I don't know what to believe about that. I just know I have to find Yun. "Why not have something to drink and stay awhile?" I say to Ming. "Maybe she'll come in."

"Luli, let's go." Ming pushes back his hair and scratches his head, clearly frustrated with me. "Yun can take care of herself. She's probably with Yong right now."

"With Yong. I know! You told me he was a kidnapper!" Mostly I say it to get a reaction from Ming. It's simpler than explaining that Yun is pregnant and scared and angry at me, and that I have to make things right.

"What are you going to do when you find her? She won't listen to you. You can't tear her away from him. You can't help her find a new position." He's still yelling. "How can you help her?"

I don't know what I'm going to do when we find her. What

she's going to do. "I just want to make sure she's okay! You're the one who told me to warn her. Will you try her mobile again?"

He huffs impatiently but pulls out his phone, taps her number, and covers his other ear so he can hear. After a moment he shakes his head and shoves the phone into his pocket. "No answer."

"Do you have Yong's number? Do know where he lives?" I'm clutching at any hope. "She's probably there if she doesn't have her things. Let's go to his place." I'll tell her I'm sorry and ask her to forget what I said. Beg her to be my friend again.

A dim light fixture overhead throws shadows on Ming's face. I can see him itching to go home. "No. And if I did, I wouldn't take you there. Maybe he's a trafficker, or maybe he just works for one, but something's shady there. I don't want any part of it. And you should stay away. Yun made her choice."

Anger shoots up in me and I feel my face grow hot. "Made her choice? You mean she didn't want *you*!"

His eyes flash, and the muscles around his mouth and on his forehead twitch, not settling into any expression. I don't know whether he's shocked, furious, or sad, but he turns away. I watch him head back to the black-painted entry alcove, elbow past the people coming through the door, and leave the club.

Right away I wish I could take back what I said. I stand watching as the clubbers stream through the door, the girls throwing off their coats to show their dressy, tight outfits. Under my shapeless black coat, the long loose sweater I wear is completely out of place. My hair gathered in a band at the back of my neck isn't pulled up high on my head or cut with sharp bangs. My cheeks and lips aren't stained red, my eyelids aren't colored glimmering blues and purples. I don't belong here without Yun or Ming.

For some reason, I don't think Ming is jealous over Yun anymore. It's me who's jealous over him. I should go after him. I don't know how to talk to him about my jealous feelings, but I can tell him I'm sorry.

I'm standing beside the door, waiting for a break in the line of people coming in so I can leave, when Yong enters the club. A small duffel is slung across his shoulder over his blue leatherette jacket with metal buckles. He nods at the bouncer and heads to the bar. There, he hands the bag to the bartender, who takes it and stashes it under the counter before getting him a beer and leaning in to speak to him. Yong props forward on his elbows. His head turns to the side as the bartender talks into his ear, the spinning dots of light crossing over his back and profile.

I've never spoken to Yong, never really met him, only seen him a few times meeting up with Yun. She's never introduced any of us girls or invited us to hang out with the two of them. He's good-looking with his square face, though now his fore-head is furrowed at whatever the bartender is saying. I wait until the bartender moves away before I edge around clubbers to approach Yong.

He is facing the bar, hovering over his beer. I stand behind him for several moments biting my lip, before I work up the nerve to speak. "Have you seen Yun?" He doesn't hear me over the music, so I tap him on the shoulder.

He twists around on his stool, his eyebrows up in a startled expression.

"Have you seen Yun?" My throat is sore from trying to talk to Ming over the music, and my raised voice sounds strained and unnatural to me. I'm not used to yelling so much.

"Yun? No. I just got back in town." His eyes move over me as he swigs his beer.

"I've been looking for her. Since yesterday. She left the factory. I don't know where she went."

"Why don't you call her?"

"No phone."

He reaches into his back pocket for his phone. "She called me a few times yesterday, but I was traveling." He dials now and holds the mobile to his ear. After a moment, he shrugs and puts his phone away. "She's not answering." He stays half turned on his stool and drinks his beer, watching the dancers.

I try to think what to say. I guess he still doesn't know about the baby, but of course, I'm not going to say anything about that. "Do you know where she could be?" I finally ask.

His eyes move left and right like he's thinking. He shifts to the edge of his stool, putting his mouth close to my ear. "She's not in her room? Out with her friends?" I can smell the beer and cigarette on his breath.

I shake my head. "She got fired yesterday. No one's seen her."

His head rolls back, and he chuffs out a noise of irritation.

"Could she be at your place?" I ask.

"I told you I've been away. And she doesn't have a key." Yong catches the bartender's eye and ticks his head toward the door. The bartender gets his bag and hands it over. Yong drains his beer, peering at me over the edge of the glass, before setting it on the bar. "What's your name?"

"Luli."

"You're from the orphanage too?"

I nod. He nods back and gets up to leave.

"Wait! Where are you going?"

"Home."

"What about Yun?"

"I'll tell her to call you if I see her." He holds up a hand in a wave and leaves.

For a moment I just stand there, again not knowing what to do. But finally I push through the crowd to follow Yong. I see him outside, strapping his bag onto his motorbike, which is parked under a streetlight just outside the nightclub. He's my best chance of finding Yun. In the back of my mind, I want to ask if I can go with him to check his place, but I hold back, not sure.

"You need a ride?"

I don't answer. I want to find Yun, but I'm a bit afraid of him.

"Come on. I'll drop you off at the factory."

I look up and down the street. It's a small side street, not many cars, but several small groups of clubbers are making their way to the restaurants and bars. I tried to pay careful attention when I walked here with Ming, and I *think* I know the way back to the factory, but I'm not certain.

Finally I say, "What about bride collecting?"

He stops working on his bag. Any hint of friendliness falls away. "What?"

I bite my lip and draw back. I can feel my heart beating in my chest, but I can't just leave it. "Yun told me you're a bride collector."

He narrows his eyes at me, his mouth a short line. "Yes."

"Some people say you"—I swallow, not wanting to say *kidnap*—"take girls to men in the countryside who pay for them."

"Husbands." He hooks the last strap onto his bag, then throws his leg over the bike. His casualness is back, as if he has nothing to hide.

"What about the girls?" I press on, even though I really just want to drop it. But I want to make sure, for Yun's sake. "Do they want to go?"

Yong sneers. "I don't make the deals. There are lots of girls from poor families. Maybe their family gets some money from the husband, or they want to unburden their family of having to feed them. It's no fun living in a starving household. Look at you and Yun—given to the orphanage. Plenty of girls need homes. Men need wives. And if they can afford to pay something, then you know they can afford to feed a family." He hops up and pushes his motorbike off its stand. "Want the ride?"

I step back, shaking my head.

CHAPTER 8

Yun

I sleep in the Taiyuan Railway Station, dozing sideways on a hard metal seat, jerking awake every few minutes when my head falls too far back. It's not much warmer here than outside—I wish for my own fluffy comforter—but at least I'm out of the wind. The huge waiting hall, as large as a factory building, echoes with the noise of people coughing, a baby crying, the occasional screech and clack of a train. This late at night the station isn't very busy. Only a few people have bags or luggage at their feet as if they're waiting to go somewhere. Most of the others are sleeping, not bothered by the fluorescent light. They probably have nowhere else to go, like me.

I'm so tired. When I can't stand it anymore, I tuck my bag into my coat and squeeze myself under the armrest that divides the seats so I can stretch out.

Next thing I know, I'm being woken by a bright flashing light. The morning sun slants directly into my face through the three-story windows.

A man with a shaven head leans over me. He bows, rocking forward and back with his hands together, muttering.

"What are you doing?!" I scream.

The man blinks, the quiet expression on his face not changing. He backs up as I scoot out from the seats and stand, pulling my coat tightly around me. He keeps up his short little bows and mumbling: ". . . those frightened cease to be afraid, and may those bound be free. May those powerless find power . . ."

I notice now that he's wearing a brown-yellow padded gown. A monk of some kind.

His words are lost to my ears as he moves on toward an old man slumped over in the next row, a spilled drink pooling under his feet.

A few people turn to us, but their attention follows the monk or drifts off to other things. The station is getting crowded now, people streaming in through the row of glass doors. I get up and smooth my coat the best I can before I go to the toilets. Once I've used the squat, washed my face at the sink, and rinsed out my mouth, I go back to the waiting hall and find a new seat.

I feel awful. A sick headache behind my eyes, the bad feeling from my stomach coming back up my throat. I remember again about the baby and press my hands against my middle.

I sit at the railway station for hours, watching the flow of people cross the waiting room. Queasy and still exhausted, my mind is mostly empty. I don't even have enough feeling to worry about the pregnancy or Yong. I know I should go over to the job market and start looking for another position, or get my things from where I left them with Gatekeeper Wu, but my legs won't get started. One by one, I pluck out hairs from the nape of my neck until I realize I've made a coin-sized bald spot. I snatch my hands away and jam them under my crossed arms. My fists are so tight I can feel my nails digging into my palms, but my hands still itch with the urge to yank at strands or at least run my finger on the smooth patch of skin.

I jump out of my seat and start pacing around the waiting hall, fingering my mobile in my pocket, pulling it out and jabbing at the numbers. It lost its charge yesterday, but I can't stop checking it.

I hadn't realized how dependent I've become on this phone. Even though I don't really want to talk to anyone except Yong, I would like to see who's tried to call me. I know a lot of people, and people call me because they know I'm usually ready to go out for snacks or to the dance clubs. Zhenzhen and Hong I see the most, but Luli is my closest friend, since she knows how it was at the orphanage.

Until Luli arrived, I felt all alone there. When she came, I had someone to talk to.

Even the last time she was shown, just before she turned fourteen and would no longer be eligible for adoption, she kept hoping. That morning, she asked me to check her for lice and comb her hair until it was slick and shiny. She put on a clean shirt she had washed herself the previous night. Then she went and sat quietly in the dayroom, waiting until she was called downstairs. In her lap, one hand rested on the other, the fingers on top fluttering every now and then to pat the hand beneath.

I thought about reminding her that people just wanted babies, or occasionally little ones. One of the caretakers had mentioned that at some of the bigger orphanages, some people—especially foreigners—were adopting older children and even handicapped children. But I'd stopped holding out hope that those foreigners would turn up in our little institute in Gujiao. I was fifteen, my documentation had never come through, and the time had come and gone for me to be shown.

Still, I didn't say anything. Later, when Luli came back to

our dayroom, her face red and streaky-wet, I patted her on the shoulder and whispered that in another year or two we would leave here. She was shock-faced then, surprised or scared, perhaps a little of both.

I'm not mad at her anymore for what she said about Yong. But she can't help me.

✦✦✦

About midafternoon at the railway station, I begin to feel better. I go outside and breathe in the smoggy-white cold, which feels as good as water splashing on my face. Across the expanse of concrete, I spot a food seller with an oil-drum stove. I buy some roasted sweet potatoes, and while I'm eating them, I decide to go back to Yong's place. He's been gone four days now, and I have the feeling that he'll be coming back soon. Besides, what else do I have to do?

When I reach his lane, I peer down it, making sure that that detective isn't there. I only see a woman's backside, shopping bags hanging from each hand. Yong's motorbike isn't where he usually parks it. Still, I go over and knock on his door several times. No answer. I move to the window and peep through a little gap between the pieces of cloth tacked up for curtains. I can't see much.

I start looking for something to get the window open. I scan the hard pack of the lane where he usually parks his motorbike, thinking maybe he left a screwdriver or some other tool. When I don't find anything, I dig into my bag and find my nail clipper. With a little scraping, I wedge its file blade between the side-by-side panes that open out like doors and pry them apart enough to get my fingers in. I yank back one side, then the other. Now I need something to stand on so that I can actually climb in. I have to go over to the next lane before I find an old crate that'll do the job.

I scramble through the window and jump down into the flat. Empty Yanjing beer bottles and Coke cans are scattered everywhere. The place smells stale and damp. Old cigarette butts overflow from ashtrays and are squashed out on the floor. Dirty laundry is piled on a stool in the corner. I heave and close my mouth tightly, trying not to take any deep breaths.

At the sink, I strip off my clothes and wash myself the best I can. I find a clean undershirt of Yong's and fall into his bed. It seems all I want to do anymore is sleep . . .

I bolt upright in bed as the door flings open and the light, a single fluorescent fixture screwed to the wall, snaps on.

"Fuck, Yun! It's you! I saw the window open! You broke into my house!" Yong slams the door behind him, drops his bag, goes to the window, and begins to crank it closed. It's dark out, though I can't say how late. The room is freezing. I pull the blankets around me.

"You're back," I say.

He goes to the table, picking up bottles, shaking them. When he finds one half full of beer, he takes a swig, then pulls a face. He locates one with Coke and drains it, before he sits at the table and lights a cigarette, gazing at me through the smoke. "So you got fired."

"How do you know?"

"I saw your friend. That one from the orphanage. What was her name? Luli?"

"Where?" I stiffen. "What did she say?"

"She's looking for you. Worried about you."

I slump back into the bed.

"Why did you get fired?" Yong asks. "Have you found another place yet? It should be easy, right?"

I nod and shrug at the same time. It *should* be easy for a young person like me to get hired on, even though Foreman Chen's words still ring in my ears. But I don't want to think about all that. Already my mind is turning to what to say about the pregnancy.

Yong finishes his cigarette and looks for a place to put it out. The ashtray's full, so he drops it into a bottle. "Well, you can find something else. One factory job is like another." He gets up, grabs a plastic bag from a shelf, and starts chucking bottles and cans into it. "How long have you been here? You could have cleaned some of this up."

"Yong, I need 450 yuan for an abortion."

The bottle in his hand drops into the bag, clanking against a can. He spins around, his head cocked like he isn't sure he heard me right.

"Fuck! What did you say?" His smooth face makes an ugly scowl around his mouth and eyes.

I flinch. Of course he's angry. My hands itch to pull on my hair, but I keep them on the blanket and steel myself, ready for an outburst, for insults. "I'm pregnant. The abortion costs 450 yuan."

He drops the trash with a clatter, bottles and cans rolling out, and puts his hands up to his head, grabbing his hair in his fists. "Shit!"

I clutch the quilt up around me. "Probably more than that with all the other tests."

He plops back onto the stool, slowly shaking his head. "How could this happen? Didn't we use the condoms? Didn't I tell you to get the birth control?"

I keep quiet, hugging my knees on the bed. My hand snakes up to my hair, pinching a lock but not plucking. We haven't *always* used the condoms. He would make a big show of using them, but if we didn't have any, he didn't mention them.

He stares at me. I drop my gaze to the old blue quilt, studying the stains and burn holes from cigarettes as I try to block all feelings. For a long time, neither of us says anything.

At last I speak. "What about the money?"

He sighs heavily and hangs his head.

"I have to get this over with," I insist. "I have to get another position."

"I just got paid, but I have to pay the rent." He kicks a can on the floor, and it skitters across the room. "How much money do you have saved?"

I think about my 532 yuan. "A hundred," I lie. "But even if I get a position tomorrow, it could be two months before I get my first pay."

He snatches up the trash bag and starts picking stuff up again. "I have to think about all this. You can stay here for now." He doesn't sound angry anymore, but there's no friendliness there either.

I'm relieved that I at least have a place to stay. I climb out of bed and realize I still have nothing clean to put on. I go over to the sink where I took off my clothes and pull on my dirty pants and coat, covering the undershirt I borrowed from Yong. I help him straighten the room before I mention that I need to get my things. He nods, not looking at me, not offering to drive me over.

I'm halfway out the door before I remember the detective. I poke my head out and peer down the dark lane. No one there. I pull back inside and shut the door. I decide I have to tell him.

If he gets caught up in something, he won't be able to help me. "Yong, someone was looking for you yesterday."

Yong's head jerks around. "Who?"

"He said he was a detective. He said he'd been trying to find you because of . . ." I bite my lips.

His eyes start the dark flashing. "What?!"

I mumble, "He was looking for some girl."

He waits for me to say more.

"I told him he had the wrong person because you're with me."

He pitches his head back, relieved. "Good. You said the right thing. The bartender at the club said he was looking for me there too."

"He didn't want me to tell you he was here. And, Yong, he thinks you're a kidnapper. He said you make women think you're their boyfriend—"

"I hope you didn't listen to any of that! Did you tell them that I'm a driver for someone else? If he's looking for someone, he should be looking for my boss. He's the one who runs the business."

Business? Bride delivery . . . or trafficking? I shut it out of my mind. "I didn't say anything. Just that he was wrong. That you're with me."

A tight smile comes to his face. "You really said the right thing. He pats the pocket of his jacket until he finds his keys. "You're with me." He holds up the keys, clacks them in his hand. "I'll go with you to get your things.

CHAPTER 9

Luli

The box of salted, dried plums bounces in my lap as the bus grinds through the city, lurching with the Sunday morning traffic. I finger the gold lettering on the clear plastic box before I go back to staring out the window. Six-lane avenues, stores and apartment buildings that span entire blocks, parks with bare trees, the leaves long fallen away. We pass through the city center, and when the streets get narrower and the buildings smaller and shabbier, I know we're getting close to Gujiao Children's Social Welfare Institute 17.

It's been two weeks since I've seen or heard from Yun. The only clue I have is that she picked up her things late in the night after Ming and I went to the Cradle Club to look for her. Gatekeeper Wu said that she had come for them when the other guard was on duty. He had no information as to where she was going or how she carried her things away or if she was with anyone. He could only say that he had found it in his generous heart to give her one more night before he chucked it all to the rag pickers. And that she was lucky she got everything when she did.

A few days after she disappeared, I bought a cell phone and got Yun's number from Ming. I've tried calling her, but the phone just rings and rings and eventually goes to voicemail. She hasn't answered my texts either. Her other friends have gotten the same treatment. They tell me that if something was really wrong—if she'd been hurt—her phone would be dead by now. The fact that the calls still go through means she's just ignoring us.

I still feel as if I'm waiting for her. That she's somewhere nearby and will get in touch with me soon. At the end of my shifts, as I walk by the other factory buildings, I always stop to scan the faces of the girls flooding out.

Ming says it's unlikely she's still at our factory working in another division. He said he was sorry for leaving me at the club, and I'm glad we've made up. But he still doesn't want to dwell on Yun. He says not to worry about her, that finding a job will probably be easy for her despite what his dad said about her being an orphan. He's sure she moved on to another factory, embarrassed that she was fired.

I want to believe him, but an embarrassed Yun does not sound like the Yun I know. And Ming still doesn't know that Yun is pregnant. Or at least that she was.

By now she must've gotten rid of the baby. Once she calmed down, I'm sure she went back to the clinic. She didn't want to keep it, and the government wouldn't allow it unless she could pay the fines for having a baby against Family Planning rules. I don't know why it makes my heart pull to think the baby is gone. I don't know why I wanted her to have it.

Lately I've been thinking more and more about the orphanage. I can't help wondering if maybe Yun went back there to see if she could get a position. Although she didn't much like taking care of the babies, it's work she knows how to do. I haven't been able to get it out of my mind.

Now, the bus pulls up to Xutan Street, close to my old elementary school. I get off and watch the bus pull away with a screech and a hiss before I start walking to the Institute. The air is thin and sharp. I hug my new coat tightly around me, glad for its coziness.

The coat is the first big purchase I've made aside from the phone. My cheap polyester coat was useless once the weather turned truly cold. So last week Ming went with me to the underground market on Bai Street. I spotted the quilted, purple coat at the third stall, but blanched and started to walk away as soon as the seller told me the price. Ming stopped me and haggled the price down by 15 yuan. "You'll have to learn. That's how it's done," he said.

Now, just outside the Institute, I stand for a moment, gripping the high collar of my coat close around my throat. At first, the gatekeeper in his box doesn't notice me. I knock on the window, and he comes out and opens the gate for me. He's the same gatekeeper who's been there for as long as I can remember, letting us in and out every day we went to school. He doesn't recognize me.

I go through and cross the courtyard toward the main building. The three stories of windows look down at me. At the second floor, near the end, where I know the dayroom to be, I expect to see Guo or one of the other Down's kids standing there, but there's only the reflection of the gray-white sky.

It doesn't feel right to enter through the big glass doors at the front of the building. I've only gone through them the first time I came to the orphanage when I was eight and then when I left.

I glance back to the gate. The gatekeeper has already gone back into his guardbox.

I go around the main building and enter at the back door near the big laundry room. The two washers and dryers are churning under the frosted windows, and a dozen colored plastic buckets sit on the floor and in the long, tiled sink, but no one is here. The hall is quiet, and I feel the chill of it, not much warmer than outside. I quickly go to the stairs.

As I reach the first landing, Caretaker Deng lumbers down from the steps above, a basket overflowing with dirty sheets on her hip. She stops on the second landing when she catches sight of me below her and peers at me from under the messy hanks of her home-cut hair. Her eyes run up and down my long coat, then to my face. I pull off my hat, and she recognizes me.

"What's this? Luli?" Of all the caretakers, Caretaker Deng was the least gruff. "Miss Luli, I should say."

Miss Luli. Her voice is laced with friendly sarcasm, and I'm embarrassed—as she intended. "How are you?" I mumble.

"What are you doing here?" She drops her basket on the landing and puts her hands on her hips, leaning back as if to relieve aching muscles.

"I . . . I just came to visit." I hold back about Yun.

"Came back to see us old folks?" Her mouth is open, amused, showing her tea-stained teeth. "Like other kids come back to see their parents, huh?" She points to the box of fancy plums I'm gripping. "What did you bring us?"

I scuttle up the steps between us and hand her the box.

She takes it with a satisfied smile as she eyes the gold lettering. "Well, I could use a break. Come on, I'll take you to visit the wards."

I follow her down the second-floor hallway, the quiet broken only by the slap, slap of her plastic shoes on the tile. We pass the baby room and then the toddlers'. I only glance in the open doors as we go by, again struck by the eerie quiet. I'd gotten used to that when I lived here—the strangeness of so many subdued children, with only the littlest ones raising a terrible noise at feeding time.

Near the end of the hall, Caretaker Deng flings open the door to the older children's dayroom. "Someone's come back to visit us!" she shouts above the noise of the television. She waves the box of salted plums in the air. Three caretakers standing at the television, sipping from jars of hot tea, tear their eyes away from the screen to look over at us. The dozen or so children see the treats and start shuffling toward us, but they're quickly shooed away by Caretaker Deng. I feel a little bad. I didn't think to bring them anything.

The caretakers crowd around me and are soon fingering my coat, asking me how much it cost, where I'm working— they know I'm working since I have such a nice coat—how much money I make. I answer all their questions while my eyes flick around them toward the children. I don't see Guo or Pengjie, who had been closest to us in age. In the back of my mind, I'm wondering about Yun, but I know without asking that she hasn't come back here. One of the caretakers would've remarked on it by now if she had. Their surprise at seeing me makes it clear that no other former wards have turned up.

After they run out of questions, the caretakers take the plums and drift back to their show. I notice now that the walls are brighter and cleaner than I remember. Though they're still the same shade of tan. All the years I was here they'd never been painted. "New paint?" I ask Caretaker Deng as she chews a salted plum.

"Yes! We had a foreign couple come here recently. The director wanted to make a good impression, so the walls got a new coat. And they actually adopted Pengjie! You remember him? They didn't mind that he was eleven years old, that he had Down syndrome. The wife's brother had Down's, and she wanted a brother for her daughter just like she had. Can you imagine?" She shakes her head as if she's never heard anything so bizarre.

She has to get back to the laundry now. She asks me if I want to visit the director, but I shake my head and say I'll go out the back way.

I follow her along the dim hallway, dumbfounded about Pengjie's amazing luck. It's hard to believe.

"Caretaker Deng, I didn't see Guo."

"He turned sixteen last month. He's in the other building now." She means the one for disabled adults.

We've reached the stairs, and Caretaker Deng hoists up her basket. "Well, it was certainly a surprise to see you come back to visit us. Every once in a while a child comes back, brought by their parents. Only the foreign ones, of course." She trudges down the stairs. "Maybe to make them feel grateful. How about you? Are you grateful you got out?"

I am, but I only incline my head slightly when she glances back at me.

"A good job in a factory! Well done! You know, I was the one that recommended you for the position in the bathroom. But you had your own mind, huh?" She stops at the bottom of the stairs, drops her basket, and leans against the railing to rest. "I honestly didn't expect you to get a better position. It's not easy to go out as a ward."

"Remember Yun? She left the year before? She helped me."

"Oh, I remember her. The one with the four pocks on her face. The two of you were always together. She got work in the factory? Really! Why didn't she come with you to see us?"

"She left the factory a couple of months ago. I lost contact with her. Actually, I was wondering if she had come back here."

Caretaker Deng frowns and shakes her head. "No. Like I said, hardly anyone comes back to visit. Huh! I understand now. You came just to ask after your friend!" She fakes a hurt look. "And I always thought you were a little different than the foundlings who grow up here."

She bends to get the basket, but I rush forward and pick it up. She grins and starts toward the laundry room as I follow.

"It's too bad your grandpa didn't release you for adoption when you first came here. Even though you were an older child, you might have actually gotten a family since you didn't have any defects."

My heart squeezes, and I quickly blink back the tears that rush up to my eyes.

"You should forget about Yun," she says as we turn into the laundry room. She raises her voice over the swish and hum of the machines. "The ones that grow up here don't know how to connect to people. Though I have to say, that girl wasn't as unlucky as everyone thought if she found a job in a factory. Why did she leave the factory?"

I shrug, unwilling to give her any reason to criticize Yun.

"Yes, you should forget her." She takes the basket from me and swings it to rest on the sink. "But I know you won't, because you had people for a while. They tried to hang onto you as long as they could, and you never forgot about them."

CHAPTER 10

Yun

Someone's calling me: a number I don't recognize. I let it go to voicemail, then listen to the message, mostly out of boredom. "Yun, it's Luli! I got a phone! Just like you kept saying I should. Anyway, I got your number from one of the other girls and I just want to check how you're doing. I know you told Dali you're okay, but where are you living? Did you—well, please call me back. I'm really sorry about what I said the last time we talked."

I swallow a lump in my throat. I'm not still angry at Luli for what she said about Yong, but I know she'll want to talk about the baby. I just can't deal with that right now.

I've been lying around Yong's for days and days, so nauseous I can barely move, too sick to hunt for a job. Yong isn't around much. He goes in and out to see friends, to work, even disappearing for a few days at time. We don't talk about the baby. I don't want to think about it, and I guess he doesn't either, although a few times I've seen him studying me, only to turn away when I notice.

He comes in now, while I'm still staring at Luli's new number debating whether to return her call. "Hey," he says. "I've been thinking. We should go to my ma's. She lives in Yellow

Grain Village, just a couple hours away. She can take care of you till we get things straightened out."

I wasn't expecting this at all. "Your ma won't mind?" None of the girls I know have met their boyfriends' parents. Most of them keep all that private, not even telling their parents that they're seeing someone. Ming definitely never introduced me to his family as his girlfriend. Certainly not his dad.

Yong shrugs. "She'll be fine with it."

I narrow my eyes at him. "If I'm going to get the termination and then find work, I should be here, in the city."

"I'll bring you back as soon as I've got enough money for it. But that could be a while, depending on how many jobs I get in the next few weeks. Don't you want to have someone looking after you in the meantime?"

Eventually, I agree. I know it might be a bad idea, but I'm too sick to care.

⬥ ⬥ ⬥

I've never been so miserable.

I cling to Yong with my head against his back. My eyes are squeezed closed against the cutting wind and dust driving into my bones. The stink of exhaust and pollution along the congested expressways nauseates me.

As we get further away from the city and into the countryside, I feel more and more uneasy. The private detective's warning flits through my mind. *He'll tell a girl they're going to go on a weekend trip together . . . then sell her . . .*

My pulse suddenly begins to speed up. For a moment I panic, wondering what I'll do if Yong isn't actually taking me to his ma's place. But Yong tears faster along the highway. The drone of the motorbike rumbles in my ears, the potholes and bumps of the smaller highways making me feel even queasier. I can yell into the wind or beat on him to stop, but then what? We're in the middle of nowhere, and it's not as if I can walk all the way back to the city. I can do nothing but hang on until he stops.

After another hour, Yong slows. We drive along the dusty, rutted road of a small township, where shabby, low-lying buildings line the main street. There are several newer, white-tiled ones interspersed—a few are even two stories high. I scan the buildings, searching for a police station, bus station, anywhere I can run to if it comes to it.

Yong turns into an alley lane and stops in front of a squat, old-style building. As I climb off the bike, I'm aware that my legs are tingling and numb from the vibration of the motor. I rub them, readying myself for whatever comes next.

Yong undoes my bags, which are piled and tied on the back of the bike, and thrusts one at me. He picks up the other two, saunters past me, and kicks at the door. "Ma! Ma! I've come home!"

I take a deep breath and quietly let it go as relief comes over me. We really are at his mother's place. He hasn't brought me to some old bachelor's home to sell me off.

The woman who opens the door has a thin face, tanned by the sun, with a network of fine wrinkles at the corners of her eyes. She's slight, but more gristly-lean than wispy. She stares at Yong, first bewildered, then cracking into a big toothy smile.

"Yong! Why didn't you tell me you were coming?" She grabs him by both forearms, scolding, but is plainly delighted to see him. I quietly let out a long breath.

"What are you doing here?" she says. "Don't you have to work? Come in, come in out of the cold." She pulls him in and, not seeing me, begins to shut the door behind him.

I hurry forward, and she notices me. The glee on her face is suspended. "Who's this?"

Yong half-turns. "Ma, she's with me."

Ma's gaze swings between Yong and me. "What do you mean?" Her hand comes off the door handle, and I quickly slip inside. It's nearly as cold inside as out.

Yong drops my bags and shuts the door, leaving us in the murky light of the single window. We're standing in a room that's barely the size of the factory dorm room, though a doorway shows another room off the side.

"Ma." He's embarrassed, awkward. I've never seen him like this. "Ma, this is Yun."

"Yun." She gapes at him—at me—at him again. "Why is she here?"

Yong rubs his arms as if warming himself. I wait, wondering what he'll say.

"Ma, we're married. She's my wife."

Ma puts her hand over her mouth, shaking her head. "What are you saying?"

I glance at Yong, not sure why he lied, but he ignores me.

"Married! How could you get the permit without your hukou?" Now I'm staring. Yong doesn't have a hukou?

Yong wipes the dust off his jacket. "It wasn't a problem." He makes a dismissive gesture with his hand. "I took care of it with a payment to the right person."

"But how long have you known each other?" Ma's hand drops to her throat. "Why haven't you brought her to meet me before?" Her voice is rising. "What kind of person . . ."

She throws a few wary glances my way until tears are running down her face. "Why didn't you ever tell me about her?" She mops at her face with her sleeve, peering at me over her arm. "What about those pocks? Don't you know those are marks of bad character?"

I stop listening. I've heard these things so many times. And I'm used to people talking about me like I'm not even there.

I move toward a red vinyl chair—the only one with any padding, though there's a large tear in the fabric—and plop into it. I'm stiff and drained from the long ride on the motorbike. There's a TV in front of the chair, and I'm tempted to turn it on to drone out Ma's moaning, but instead I take in the house.

Besides the three mismatched chairs near the TV, the room is crowded with a large cupboard, a table with stools near the brick stove, and a bed at the back of the room. A faded flowered sheet hangs partly across it, acting as a privacy curtain. The dresser wedged in at the foot of the bed is covered with a little shrine: photos, candles, incense poking out of a gold-colored pot, and a bouquet of plastic flowers. Around the room, a calendar and several pictures of nature scenes are pasted to the wall. There's one frame with several small photos crowded behind the glass. Yong and another boy who looks slightly older. Now I start to understand. Yong must be a second child, born in violation of Family Planning policies. That's why he doesn't have a hukou.

It strikes me that Yong has told me very little about himself.

Yong falls into the chair beside me and snaps on the TV, turning it way up. Ma, still bawling him out, moves to the stove and begins clattering her pots. She makes so much noise for such a little person.

"How long can you stay?" Ma shouts at Yong.

"I have to leave tomorrow, get back to work."

Ma bangs a pot onto the table. "So soon! Why did you come here then? For just one day!"

"Yun's going to stay here with you." Yong yells over his shoulder. "I'm leaving her here with you."

I look at Ma. She stands frozen in disbelief; her hand is on the pan she just banged against the table. "You're leaving her here?" Her mouth turns deeply to a frown.

"I have to go back to work."

"How are you going to make a son if you're in the city and she's here?"

"Don't worry, Ma. I'm sure I've put a boy inside her."

Ma's head turns sharply to me, her mouth a small round circle of surprise, and her bad temper vanishes.

I, on the other hand, feel as if Yong has dumped cold water on me. Does Yong actually want me to have this baby? Or is he just saying that so his mother will be willing to take me in? I can't tell, and in this tiny house, I may not get a chance to ask him.

Not that he'd tell me the truth.

For the first time, it fully sinks in: I can't trust Yong. And now I'm stuck here, in the middle of nowhere, with hardly any money and no guarantees about what will happen next.

I don't want to break down in front of Yong. Luckily, I'm so exhausted that I don't even have the energy to cry.

CHAPTER 11

Luli

Dali and I are lucky to find seats in the middle of the crowded classroom—really just an office on the second floor of an old building a few blocks from the factory. Potential students, still stuffed in their coats, pack the room, crowding the sides and jammed into the chairs behind the long, narrow tables, a couple of girls even trying to share their seats. I don't mind the crush because being squeezed between Dali and some girl on my other side helps me to stay propped on my stool. I've worked overtime all week, and all I can think about is stretching out on my bunk and going to sleep.

Beside me, Dali leans forward, listening intently to the instructor. Like many of the girls I work with, Dali somehow seems to have energy to do things after the long hours of work. But instead of noodles, karaoke, and hair washes, she takes classes, trying to improve herself. She's already taken classes in typing and English. She moved into my dorm building several months ago, and whenever I go to her room to see if she's heard anything about Yun, she always talks to me about taking classes, developing myself, moving up in the factory. She pushed me to go with her to this free information session. She was so hopeful that I agreed.

"In this course, you will learn how to attain your goals and achieve a higher position by developing confidence and correct etiquette." In a suit jacket and red tie, the instructor is the only person here who's taken off his coat. The room isn't heated, and his hands, as he tugs at the lapels of his blazer, are red and chapped with cold. "How you present yourself is very important, and you will learn how to make the most of your appearance." He pauses, and his gaze travels across the room. Dali's hands slip up to smooth back her staticky hair. She always has a roommate cut her hair to save money, same as me.

"If you want to achieve your goals, you must mold yourself into the type of person who exhibits quality. It is this type of person who will gain the coveted positions." The instructor gestures lightly with an open hand. "Most of you would like to move up to office positions, become a clerk or secretary, perhaps a sales associate. To stand out, the most important skill is outward confidence. With the attainment of confidence, you will be able to tackle any task of the position you have won."

The air in the room stirs as we all lift our chins, and those standing make themselves taller.

Raise competitiveness, display eloquence, build enthusiasm, boldly express oneself. The instructor continues his speech. I feel all the more weary as he talks. I hunch in my seat, studying my callused fingertips.

I think of Granddad's hands—rough, thin fingers reaching out from his sickbed to pat me on the shoulder when I told him I had pulled the bean stalks and fed the goats. What was it that Caretaker Wu said the other week back at the orphanage? *You had people.*

The *wheak* of Dali's nylon coat rubbing against mine swipes

Granddad from my thoughts. She's standing up now, smoothing her hair back again, and clearing her throat. "My dream is to achieve a position as a secretary for a department head of a large factory."

The class claps. I can't help being impressed by Dali's *confidence* and *eloquence*. She slides her eyes over to me, a pleased look on her face.

"And what about you?" the instructor asks. "What do you hope for in the future?" He's looking at me.

My face flushes hot. I feel stuck in place.

Dali nudges me. "Stand up!"

I slowly rise. I'm suddenly too warm in my coat.

"Now, tell us what your goal is in life."

My mind is blank white as I stand there, everyone looking at me, waiting for me to say something. The instructor, Dali, all these girls with their lipsticked mouths and fur-lined hoods hanging down their backs. . . .

"Speak up now. *Express yourself with boldness!* What is your hope?"

The rows of blue-shirted factory workers bent over tables, Granddad's farm, finding Yun—they all wheel in my mind. I can only open and close my mouth like a fish in a tank.

"You want to be successful? Leave the numbing life of the assembly line and gain a higher position and salary?" The instructor raises his chin as if willing me to *achieve confidence* and speak. "Because only with your own decisive action will you raise yourself up and help your family attain a higher station in life!"

I have no family, but *raising myself up* is something to think about. I latch to that idea and give a vigorous nod, and finally the instructor moves on to the next person.

It's almost eleven by the time the free seminar concludes. Dali signs on to take the course. Although she usually hates to part with money, she boldly counts off 140 yuan and hands it to the instructor. She elbows me, encouraging me to sign up as well, but I only shake my head. I haven't brought any money, and anyway, I'm still not sure.

We walk out into the frosty night. Light spills from the store signs and street lamps. It's quiet except for people who attended the seminar trickling out of the building. My mind is full of the strangeness of the meeting. It was a change from the mind-dulling work of the factory. I think of the other girls' shiny, eager expressions. *Interested.* They all wanted more.

What is your hope? At the Institute, I longed first for Granddad to come back for me, then for a new family, but neither happened. After that, I hoped for a good job, which I have now. Since I started working, I haven't really thought about what more I want.

"I think it will be worth it!" Dali says, her teeth flashing. "I send home enough to my ma, and I don't spend anything on myself, except for things that *will lift me up.*"

"I was surprised at how quickly you *achieved confidence.*" The words feel strange on my tongue. "You spoke up so . . . *confidently.*" I can't think of any other word.

"I've taken other classes like this. They always start with that stuff. You have to discover and develop yourself to stand out and move forward." She sounds so much like the instructor that I laugh.

Dali shrugs. "Well, you certainly were tongue-tied when you had to speak about your future. Your face was as red as candied crab apple! But it's okay, I was the same way the first time I had to speak in front of people. It can be so uncomfortable! It gets easier, though. Did you get any ideas about what you want to do with your life?"

I shrug. "I guess I'd like to get married. Have a family." I can't help thinking of Ming. Lately he's started trying to kiss me, and I've almost decided to let him . . .

"What!" Dali stops in the street under the glare of a yellow streetlight. "Luli, that's so old-fashioned. That's what my mother is always pushing. *Find someone, get married, give me a grandchild*! You'd think she'd be happy that I'm making money to help pull the family up, but no . . ."

I wince, and she claps her hand over her mouth as if she just remembered that I have no family. "Sorry!" She drops her hand, and we start walking again. "I see," she says after a moment, her voice quiet. "I can't imagine what it's like without a family."

Back at the factory, as we near our dorm, I see someone perched on a concrete bench in the plaza. The floodlights shine harshly on his face, and my heart skips. It's Ming. He's waiting for me.

He stands up when he spots me. I rush over to him, waving good night to Dali as she heads into the building.

Up close, I see that the skin around one of his eyes is red and puffed.

"What happened?" I ask, reaching toward his eye.

He flinches and pulls back. "I got in a fight."

"A fight? With who?"

He scowls. "Yong."

"Yong!" I cry out in surprise, my voice echoing through the whole courtyard. "Where? Did he say anything about Yun?

Does he know where she is? Why did you fight?" My breath comes out in white puffs.

"Shhh! She's fine." He huffs. "She's gone to the country-side. Staying with his ma."

I'm instantly alarmed. I know Yun wouldn't want to live in the countryside. "Are you sure he was telling the truth? What if he's sold her?"

Ming shakes his head. His mouth is an angry slash. "She's pregnant with Yong's kid. He won't sell her if he thinks she's going to give him a son."

I let out my breath. So she hasn't had the abortion. And if Yong has promised to take care of her, maybe Yun *would* agree to leave the city. I try to let go of the fear that she's been taken against her will. "Does she still have her phone? Can we call her?"

Ming's eyes narrow. "You don't seem surprised that she's having a baby. Did you know already?"

I bite my lip and nod slowly. I've been telling myself that the baby isn't any of his business, but really I've kept quiet about it because I didn't know how he would handle the news. If he's still not over Yun . . . He stares at me. Guilt that I held back information jumbles with old jealousy as I wait for him to react.

He rolls his eyes up to the sky. The smog high above is even visible at night, lit gray by the lights of the city. "Well, she's fine," he says again. "You've been crazy wondering about her, so I thought I'd tell you right away."

"Is that all you know?"

Ming shrugs. "What more do you need to know? I found out where she is for you. Got this"—he puts his face near mine and points to his eye—"for persisting when that useless piece of shit didn't want to tell me anything."

I can see that he expects me to appreciate the trouble he went to, the risk he took. And I do. But something about his tone reminds me of the caretakers at the Institute. Always calling us ungrateful, making us feel small.

I take a deep breath. "Can we call her?" I ask again.

Ming shakes his head in disgust. "I don't want you to talk about her anymore. Not to me, anyway. You don't owe her anything, you know. She hasn't called you. She doesn't care enough about you to even contact you! What kind of friend is that?"

I blink back the tears that threaten to push out. Ming doesn't know Yun like I do. "We were together seven years at the Institute. She was the only one there who helped me or showed me any kindness. To me, she's like family."

Ming sighs, and the harshness leaves his voice. "Luli, you just have to go on with your own life. You're not responsible for Yun." He opens his arms. "I'm the one you should care about."

I slip my arms around his waist and lean against him. But I'm still worried about Yun in the countryside.

CHAPTER 12

Yun

By late January, my belly seems as large as a watermelon. The baby is restless inside me like an upset stomach. It moves around a lot, but each time it does, I'm surprised. And alarmed that I've let things go so long. When I first got here, I thought I would have an abortion and go back to work within a month, but time keeps ticking by. Yong hasn't come back or sent any money. He hasn't even texted me in weeks.

I clamp my hands over my stomach. I should've known Yong wouldn't come through, that he wouldn't actually pay for the procedure. I should've figured out another plan by now. But I've been lulled into not doing anything because I've felt so sickly and Ma insists on taking care of me.

Yong's ma comes into the house, letting in a flash of winter light as she opens and shuts the door. She sees me at the table, holding my belly. "Is he moving?" Her eyes are greedy for the baby as she pulls off the woolen hat she wears, a castoff of Yong's or his brother's. Her thin cheeks are chapped red from the wind.

I shrug and move my hands away from my middle, placing them around the hot cup of tea I'm drinking.

"Not much longer now." Ma grins. "He'll be here a few weeks after Spring Festival."

Ma is sure it's a boy. Months back, when she saw that I was nauseous every day, for most of the day, she declared, "Sick all day means a boy! When I got pregnant the second time, I was so sure it was a boy, we decided we would pay the fines instead of having an abortion. I just knew it was another boy, because of how sick I was. I've been very lucky!" Her eyes stole over to me, lighting on the pocks on my face, and she sighed. By then I knew the rest of the story. Yong's father died before they paid the fines, and Yong never got his hukou.

Now, Ma tears her eyes away from my belly. She goes to the big cupboard, rummages in a sack of potatoes, and brings out three fat sweets. "Come over here," she says as she moves to the stove. "I want to show you how to cook these. You have to learn how to cook and take care of things. Come on. We have to get ready for Wei."

Wei is Yong's older brother. He works as a cleaner in a plastics factory in Quingxu. Ma told me that he's not been able to find a good position because he doesn't meet the minimum height requirements of most of the factory jobs. He doesn't make very much money.

Ma hums as she scrubs the potatoes. "I don't know what he's thinking, coming home this time of year. He shouldn't take time off. His boss shouldn't let him off. It's too close to the Spring Festival. *That's* the time to come home." Even as she rails against him, she talks cheerfully and peels and chops with quick, light movements. She doesn't seem to care that I just stand there watching instead of doing anything myself. "See, see." She pauses to show me how to hold the knife. "I know you know how to work. You worked so hard in that factory. Now you have to cook the baby." She elbows my belly gently and laughs.

I can't help but chuckle too, not at what she said about the baby, but at Ma herself. Ma's not bad to me. She actually takes pretty good care of me. She makes me special teas and broths, pushes me to eat all the time. I used to go with her to the market and help her with the fieldwork, but she made me stop once I started to get big, even before the growing season was over. Now she only asks me to do light chores around the house. And if I don't do them, she doesn't yell at me.

The door opens and bangs shut. "Ma!"

We turn to see Wei standing there. Ma bolts over to him, clucking and patting and swiping the dust off him. He isn't much taller than Ma. He stands slumped forward, clearly worn out. His hair looks like it's been buzzed by a roadside barber.

As soon as she settles, Ma ticks her head toward me. "Your brother's wife."

Wei shakes off an overnight bag slung on his shoulder and hands it to Ma. He nods at me, unsmiling. "Your husband's been arrested."

The baby rolls inside me.

Ma drops Wei's bag as she lets out a strangled cry. Her hands fly up to her face. "What are you talking about?"

Wei moves to the coal heater in the middle of the room and puts his hands near it to warm them. "They say he's abducted someone." He stares through the open hole at the red glowing coals. "Yong says that he's been mistaken for his boss. That his boss tricked him." He throws a glance at us over his shoulder. "He needs money to get out."

Ma rushes over to Wei and clutches his arm. She starts crying and drilling him with questions. I stop listening. Blood roars in my ears. *Bride collecting.*

"Yun! Yun!" Ma shouts at me. She and Wei are both looking keenly at me. "Do you have any money?"

My mind flies to the 532 yuan hidden in the lining of my comforter. I thrust it out of my mind and shake my head, keeping my face as plain as millet porridge.

Ma rushes around the room, going through her bag and a small crock where she keeps loose change. "I only have what you boys send me. So little! I've been using it all to buy good food for the baby. How much do we need?"

Wei crosses his arms and leans against the stove. "Not sure. As much as you can get."

Ma stops counting her wrinkled bills and coins. She lowers her voice. "You think they'll take a bribe?"

"Yong thinks it's more likely than getting bail. Faster."

Ma's face crumples. She grips her money in her hands and clasps them together, moaning into them. Wei and I look at each other. His eyes jump briefly to my belly. I don't know what to make of his look. His eyes and mouth seem neither angry nor sad, and of course, there's no happiness in them. I wonder if he believes me about the money.

♠♠♠

All night, the baby churns and churns as if it wants to break out. My sleep is fitful. By dawn the baby has settled on my bladder and when I can't hold my water any longer, I crawl out of the warm blankets, slip on my coat and shoes, and walk to the communal squats at the end of the lane.

The air on my face is as sharp as knives. The cold, wet air and the blotchy, metal-colored sky make me think it might snow later. I hope it holds out until Ma has borrowed enough money to send Wei back to Gujiao to get Yong out, even though I'm not sure I really want Yong to come here. We haven't felt like an actual couple since I told him I was pregnant. I don't think about him the way I used to. I don't feel any hunger to be with him.

After I piss and leave the toilets, I see Wei coming down the lane, one gloveless hand shoved in his pants pocket. The other hand holds a cigarette. He draws on it, then coughs. The white puffs streaming out of his mouth are made larger by his breath in the cold.

I hesitate. He sees me and makes a gesture for me to wait as he strides over.

"I thought you might be here. I wanted to talk to you alone." He takes another drag on the cigarette before he drops it and coughs out another stinking white cloud. "The baby, do you know if it's a boy or girl?"

His question catches me off guard. "Your mother and Yong think it's a boy."

"How do they know? Did you have an ultrasound to determine the sex?"

I shake my head. "The doctor I saw said that's illegal."

He glances around like he's afraid someone is listening. But there's no one around except a few chickens scratching at the weeds by the side of the lane. There are some clinics and mobile vans that will tell you for a big fee. But I guess you have to know where to find them.

He coughs again, bringing up a wad of phlegm. He twists around and spits it out behind him. "Yun"—he says my name as if we're old friends, but it sounds strange to my ears—"I'm going to find a way to get Yong out of jail. But you know it's all true."

He's standing less than five feet from me. His eyes are troubled. They rove past me to the alley walls, the gravel under foot, the leaden sky.

"He isn't the main one who finds the girls. I don't think he knew about it when he first started. He really was just a driver for his boss at first. But he definitely knows everything that's going on now." He sighs. "I don't know what happened to my little brother. All he cares about is money these days. Ever since he went to the city. He couldn't get a good job in the factories because he doesn't have the hukou. Eventually he found work with this boss, got a taste of nightclubs and motorbikes and money. Romancing girls and tricking them, taking them to the countryside and selling them." He tracks a scattering of black birds as they fly overhead, cawing and beating away the dead of the morning. "He'll do anything for the money. It's the money that's changed him."

I have nothing to say to that. I know what it's like to feel that you have no options. But it seems to me that even without a hukou, Yong was better off than I was growing up. He's always had a home, a good mother, an unblemished face. I can't find it in my heart to pity him.

Wei sighs. "But he's my brother and I have to get him out for Ma. He's going to come back here. When the baby is born, if it's a boy, he'll want to keep it. But if it's a girl . . ." His eyes are grim.

"If it's a girl, what?"

"Maybe he'll want to sell her."

Sell a girl? I think of all those kids in the Institute. The baby girls with nothing wrong with them except that they weren't boys. "Why would anyone want to pay for a girl? People can just get a girl from an orphanage."

Wei shakes his head. "It's actually not that easy if you can't afford to pay the required 'donation' to the orphanages. Even though people here are getting richer, those fees are way too high. And apparently, since that earthquake in Sichuan last year, there's been a huge spike in demand. Thousands and thousands of people lost their kids, and now they're desperate to adopt because they're too old to get pregnant again."

I don't know how to feel about this. It sounds heartless to sell a baby. But really, I don't want this baby anyway. If it's sold to a good home, so much the better. Still, the fact that Yong thinks that he could decide this for me makes me angry. It must've been his plan from the beginning, and instead of telling me, he let me believe he'd help pay for the abortion.

I never should've trusted him.

Wei glances around again. The lane is still empty. "I know you and Yong aren't married."

I cross my arms and try to rub off the cold. "So? It doesn't bother me. Yong just told your mother that so she wouldn't lose face."

"But don't you get it? If you're not his wife, there's nothing to stop him from . . ."

He trails off, letting the rest go unspoken. Now it sinks in what he's trying to tell me.

Yong might sell me too.

Probably to some distant farmer who needs someone to make a baby, take care of him, work in the fields.

I haven't been unhappy here in the country with Ma taking care of me. But I am not going to be the drudge of some stinking farmer too old or ugly to find himself a wife.

I've got to get away before Yong comes back.

CHAPTER 13

Yun

I go back to the house and sit at the table while Ma makes breakfast. Wei comes in, and we eat without looking at each other. The room is filled with Ma's sharp sighs and clutching breaths as she lists everyone they're going to try to borrow money from. I can feel Wei studying me, but I don't pay any attention.

My mind is trying to sort out what to do. The only thing I can think about is getting out.

Ma and Wei rush out of the house, leaving me to wash the breakfast dishes. As soon as they're gone, I pull my money out of the comforter and push it into the pocket of my jeans. The jeans sit low on my hips, held together with an old belt Ma found because I can't snap the button or pull up the zipper all the way. But my coat and big sweater cover the gap between my shirt and pants. I stuff my comforter into one of my bags and grab the others, which I never really unpacked. When I stick my head out the door, the alley is empty.

I walk to the bus station.

The man behind the single ticket window says the bus to Gujiao won't arrive until 11:55. I pay the 8 yuan for the ticket and lumber over to a chair in the corner, away from the window. The room is small and dingy, with only a single, rumpled poster advertising tours to Píngyáo, *ancient preserved city, a UNESCO World Heritage Site!* The ticketing agent eyes my fat stomach and the bags around my feet before he reaches over and slides the glass shut with a bang.

There are no other people in the bus station. I can hear the tick of the clock that hangs over the ticket window.

Now I have to think about where to go next. Train station, health clinic, job center? Who will hire me now? I curse myself for not taking care of this baby earlier.

I tug at the fine hair behind my ears, feeling the pinch. I first came to Ma's with a bare spot in the underside of my longer hair. When she saw what I was doing she begged me to stop, and every time she caught me pulling, she put a mug of tea or a piece of fruit in my hand. But now the old urge is back. I try being satisfied with just twisting or tugging on a lock.

More than two hours pass. I still haven't decided what I'm going to do when I get to Gujiao.

The station door sweeps open.

"When you get to Jiaocheng, try to get my cousin to go to his neighbors if he doesn't have any money himself. After that, call Lau's father again. I'll check in with him every day. And if you still don't have enough, try your brother's friends in Gujiao!"

I recognize Ma's shivery voice even though she and Wei both have their faces half buried under scarves and hats. I let go of my hair and ball my fists in my lap, frozen.

Wei waves at her to stop talking as they step toward the ticket window. She hovers beside him, watching as he buys a ticket, not seeing me. I think about slipping out and waiting somewhere else. I wonder if gathering my bags will attract their attention.

When the ticket agent shuts the window and Wei starts counting his change, Ma goes on giving him instructions. "Try the bribe first. That would make everything so much easier! Tell them about the baby coming. If they're unsure about taking a bribe, this will make them feel better about it. I'll keep raising money in case they're too greedy."

Wei turns, nodding absently as he stuffs his wallet in his pocket. He glances up and sees me.

The look on his face makes Ma turn around. Her eyes go first to my stomach, then to my bags cluttered around my legs. "Yun! What are you doing here?"

I glance at Wei and decide not to say anything.

"What are you doing?" Ma asks again.

I clamp my lips together and shift my gaze to the blue plastic chairs across the room.

Ma comes to my corner and plants herself in front of me. "What's going on? Why are you here? With all your bags?" Her eyes travel back and forth across my face, but I still don't answer.

Her baffled expression clears suddenly, and she throws up her hands as if she understands everything. "Oh, you're a good girl!" She laces her fingers and joggles her clamped hands toward me. "But I don't think you can do anything." Instantly unsure, she wheels around to Wei. "Do you think it will help if she goes with you?" She doesn't wait for him to answer before she spins back to me. "But the baby! It's too much for you and the baby. You shouldn't go anywhere!" She bends over and starts gathering my bags.

I quickly reach down and try to grab the straps out of her hand. We have a brief tug-and-pull until I set my teeth and snatch them free. Ma straightens up, her mouth drawing down in a frown. I turn away. "What's wrong with you?" she asks.

I won't look at her.

"She's running away," Wei says.

"What are you talking about?" Ma's voice rises so sharply, the man behind the ticket window glances up from behind the glass.

"Ma . . ." Wei starts, but breaks off.

"What is it? Why are you leaving, Yun?"

I still don't answer her. It seems too much trouble to explain that her son is a black-hearted devil. I just want to be done with them.

Ma begins shaking. "What do you think you're doing? You can't go anywhere!" She balls her fists and stamps her thighs with them. "You can't take our baby!"

My ears get hot. I clench my teeth to hold back a curse.

Ma instantly seems to think better of her outburst. She perches on the chair beside me, picks up my hand, and starts rubbing it. Her hand is warm and strong against my cold one. "Now, you heard Wei. This is all a mistake. Come back home with me. Nothing to worry about. Wei will get Yong out and bring him home to us. He'll find another job. Stop this and come home with me." She forces a big smile and looks at me expectantly. I pull my hand out of her grasp and fold both hands together under my belly.

Ma turns to Wei, not understanding, pleading. "Wei?" He has only a blank face to give her.

"Wei! We can't let her go! She can't just run off!"

Ma rises and rushes to the ticket agent's window. She raps on it so hard, the glass shakes on its track.

The ticket agent slides it open, scowling at her. Ma shouts at him, "Call the police! I need to have my son's wife detained. She's trying to run away, but she's about to have his baby!"

I curse, jump up, and grab my bags.

"Wei! Stop her!" Ma flaps her hands at him to move.

Hesitantly, Wei steps toward me and tries to take my bags. I brush past him and head toward the door, but Ma flies at me and grabs me. "Wei! Wei!"

He grabs my other arm, but his grip is unconvincing. I thrash, trying to jerk away, which makes him hang on to me more tightly. Ma's frail body lurches against me and my bags. One bag comes unzipped. Clothes and makeup scatter. My comforter spills out and sweeps the floor.

The ticket agent slams down the phone and bustles out into the waiting room. "Settle down now! Settle down!" He's taller than Wei by a head. With a swift motion, his hands lock onto my upper arms, pressing them against my sides. Wei lets go, but Ma moves with us.

"Calm down! That's enough of all this." The ticket agent brings me back to the chairs in front of the window and pushes me to sit. Ma, still holding on to me, lowers herself beside me. "All this will be sorted out when the police get here." The ticket agent lets go of me and steps back.

I jump up again and, still holding my half-empty bags, yank my arm out of Ma's grip. The force of it causes me to strike her in the chin. She cries out.

"Now you've done it! You've hit your mother-in-law!" The ticketing agent skirts around me and gets hold of me from the back and side.

I can feel his hot breath on my forehead. I turn my head and spit in his face. His mouth drops open in shock. "Lunatic!" His arms lock tighter around me, his eyes narrowing into angry slits.

"Be careful of the baby!" Ma wails.

I fight as hard as I can, twisting, flailing, dropping my bags and trying to kick, but my big stomach makes it hard to raise my legs. Wei steps forward and gets hold of both my wrists. The ticket agent squeezes me harder and tighter the more I struggle, until I can hardly move and am gasping for breath. Blood pounds in my head. I can hear Ma bleating, "Yun! Yun! Please stop! The baby! The baby!"

"What kind of girl is this?" the ticket agent hisses in my ear. His breath comes out in short pants. "You have a real problem with this one!"

No one answers. I will Wei to look at me, but he keeps his eyes averted. He looks weak and miserable.

The station door bursts open. Two women and a man in thick coats crowd into the waiting room, plastic bags and suitcases dragging in their arms.

"Move over there." The ticket agent calls out to them. From the corner of my eye I can see him point with his chin.

The travelers shuffle over a few steps but fan out in front of us, gaping openly. The man asks the ticket agent, "What's all this about?"

"Family problems. Go over there. I'll be with you in a minute."

A moment later a police officer enters the station. "What's going on?"

Ma turns her pleading gaze to him. "My daughter-in-law! She's running away. You can see she's pregnant."

The police officer looks at me—at the bulge of my stomach, at my coat straining at the zipper, up at my face. He studies my pocks for a moment before he abruptly turns to Wei. "Why's your wife running away?"

Wei drops my hands. "She's not—"

Ma breaks in, "My other son's wife. He's . . . in the city."

"I'm not his wife!" I spit out.

Ma's face contorts with grief. "Why are you lying like this?" She turns to the police officer. "She's not well. She had some bad news about my son. You can see she's pregnant with my grandchild."

I shake my head fiercely. "No, no. We never married! This isn't even his child. It's not!"

"Yun! Don't say that!" Ma screams.

The cop asks Ma, "Do you have the marriage certificate?"

"No. It's with my son, my other son. But he's in the city. This one"—she gestures to Wei—"was just leaving to bring him here. Yun's been living with me for the last several months."

The officer waves his hands at the ticket agent. "Let go of her. Take care of your other customers." He thumbs toward the office.

"Careful," the ticket agent warns. "She was fighting like a wild animal. Punched her mother-in-law. Even spat in my face." He slowly loosens his grip on me, backs away, and goes into the office.

I gulp air deep into my lungs as the cop gestures for the travelers to go to the ticket window. They reluctantly shift their eyes away when the ticket agent slides the window open.

The officer holds out his hand to me. "Your ID card?"

I drop into a chair and lean back for a moment, drawing in several breaths and rubbing the sides of my belly. It feels rigid and clenched. Ma's hands are pressed over her mouth, her eyes as large as eggs. She's worrying about the baby. All she cares about is the baby.

I reach to get my bag, but she hastily scoops it up and hands it to me. I dig around until I find my card.

The cop studies it. He raises his brow to me. "You're only just eighteen. Too young for marriage."

Ma opens her mouth, but nothing comes out. She leans in to peer at my ID card, but I know she can hardly read.

"Having a child out of wedlock is a violation of Family Planning regulations."

Ma jumps in, "There must be some misunderstanding. She's twenty! This card is some sort of trick. I'm sure my son has their marriage papers. Let me take her home. Wei here is going to pick up Yong. As soon as he's back we'll get it all sorted out."

The cop slowly runs his tongue over his teeth, the bulge of it pushing out the skin around his lips. "I think I'd better take her to the station. Fighting, running away, pregnant but unmarried, mentally unstable? Something's not right. We'll keep her there for the time being—until your sons get home at least."

Ma is thinking, her eyes shifting back and forth. She nods. "Good. Good. Wei will bring my son, *her husband*, back and we'll get it all sorted out. And nothing will happen to the baby?"

The officer twitches his head dismissively. He slips my ID card into the breast pocket of his coat and points at my scattered possessions. "Take all this home with you," he says to Ma.

Wei and Ma start picking up my things while the officer takes hold of my arm and pulls me to the door.

Just before he pushes me out into the stinging cold, Ma straightens up and calls to me. "I'll visit you later—bring you something to eat! Please take care of my grandson!"

CHAPTER 14

Yun

The police station is a two-room, low-ceilinged building a short walk away. In the front room, the cop steers me past a large, black metal desk where another officer sits behind a computer, slurping his lunch. He starts to put his bowl down, but my cop gestures for him to keep eating as he pulls open a connecting door.

Inside the second room, two small cells face a long narrow window high above. My heart begins to race and the baby inside me kicks and turns. I stop, my heels digging in, but the officer pulls me forward.

In the first cell, a middle-aged man sits on the low platform that runs along the back wall. He looks at me, my pocks, my belly, staring flatly as we pass. With his battered blue coat and the stubble along his jawline, he could be anyone squatting by the side of the road waiting for a bus.

The cells share a solid wall between them. We pass to the second one. The cop hesitates, glancing at my stomach. But after a moment he thrusts a key into the lock, pushes open the heavy bars, and motions me in with a flip of his fingers.

There's a sitting board along the wall and a bucket in the corner, which, from the smell of the place, serves as the toilet.

The baby turns inside me again, feeling so heavy. I move to sit. The board is just a few inches off the floor. My pants feel like they're going to split apart. The cop watches me with a little frown, and it strikes me that he's troubled by the conditions of the cell because of the baby. But he clanks the door shut, locks it, and leaves.

Although it's nearly as cold inside as it was outside, my armpits and the back of my neck began to feel damp. I see the metal bars, the spaces between, the peeling green paint on the wall. It's the same paint they used in the orphanage. Blood rushes up to my ears. I try to get up from the sitting board, but I've forgotten my size and only fall back.

"What's your charge?" The man speaks to me from the other cell.

I don't answer. I'm not sure myself what I've done wrong. Is being pregnant and unmarried enough to get me locked up?

"Second child?" he guesses. "He'll be calling in the Family Planning officials."

People are always so nosy. I just keep quiet.

He sighs wearily. "My neighbor said I was trying to steal his pigs. It was a dispute between us, and I got the bad end of it, because I didn't have any money to pay a bribe. Have they processed you yet?"

I was planning to just ignore him, but now I'm wondering what he means. His voice is not unkind. "Process?"

"Get your information. Have you signed papers?"

The cop still has my ID card, but I haven't signed any papers. "No."

"That's good. Get your people to come here and offer to pay a fine. Before he gets Family Planning involved. If you come up with some money right away, it will probably cost you less. It won't get you the household registration papers for the baby, but they might leave you alone so you can try to raise the money for it."

I think of the money in my jeans—532 yuan, minus the bus ticket. And there's still time to catch the bus. I have the ticket in my coat pocket. I have to get out of here no matter what. I scramble up clumsily and start yelling for the cop: "Officer! Officer! Officer!"

The door to the room scrapes open. "What's going on? What's the noise about?"

The bars are cold as ice on my cheek as I push my face against them. I thrust my arm out, waving at the officer. He's the same one who brought me in. He swipes his mouth with the back of his hand, chewing. He must have just started eating his lunch.

"I want to pay my fine!"

He stalks over to my cell. "What's this?"

"I want to pay my fine. I have money!"

He frowns. "But I haven't charged you with anything yet." He swallows whatever's left in his mouth and tips his head to one side. "Your family was going to get your . . . husband—"

"He's in jail in Gujiao!" My mind races. I already told him that I wasn't married to Yong. He probably hasn't checked my ID number yet and is still confused about my status. "And my family doesn't have any money! They were borrowing money to get him out of jail in the city." If only he would just take the money and let me go . . .

I pull up my coat, dig cash out of my pants pockets and hold it out to him. "Let me pay this! Please!"

He looks thoughtfully at me, then at the money. I thrust the money at him, willing him to take it.

"You should let her pay now." My cellmate moves to his

bars. I can see his hands wrapping around them. "Don't involve the Family Planning Council. They'll force her to abort and make her pay for it. Or charge her with huge fines if she keeps the baby. She'll never get out from under the weight of that debt." He still thinks I'm breaking the one-child policy, but the truth is that I'll be loaded down with fines all the same. This fills me with so much panic that I feel dizzy.

"Besides, she might have that baby any moment."

I see the chance my cellmate is giving me. I grip my belly, double over with a gasp, and fake a pain.

"You stay out of it!" The officer points a finger at my cellmate.

Clutching my stomach with one hand, I push the money at him again. "Please, Officer!"

"She says her family won't have the money to pay those big fines." My cellmate ignores the officer's order. "Her man is in jail. Let her pay what she has and be done with it, eh? No one has to know anything about it. She'll go to the city. Let it be their problem. You see those unlucky marks on her. Better to get those pocks out of here."

The officer's eyes turn to me, and I can feel the flicker of them—one, two, three, four—as they jump from one pock to another. He grabs the money, shoves it into his pocket, and takes out the key. As he opens the cell door and hands me my ID card, he keeps his eyes averted, like I don't exist.

I bolt out of the cell. As I pull open the door to the outer room, I half-turn toward my cellmate. He nods at me. I tick my head back at him and go. I don't know why he decided to help me, but I'm not going to waste the chance he's given me.

✦✦✦

Out on the street, the icy wind blasts trash and dust every which way. There's less than an hour until my bus arrives, but I know I can't wait inside the station because Wei might still be there, waiting for his bus to Jiaocheng. I don't want to take the chance of going into any of the shops or restaurants either because it seems like everyone knows each other in the village. Instead, I hide in an alley stamping my feet and breathing into my hands, hoping no one will notice me. Luckily, the freezing temperature keeps people inside or hurrying along the streets with their heads tucked under their hoods.

Finally, I hear the screech of the bus pulling to a stop. I peer around the building. Two passengers get on. I wait a few moments more before I dart aboard. I thrust my ticket at the driver, find a seat near the front, and slide down as much as my big stomach allows.

The door shuts, and the bus starts off. I sigh. My fingers find the back of my neck, and I begin to yank out strands of hair. I realize I haven't needed my old habit these last few months at Ma's. Now, all my things are gone. I have no money. I have a baby that I don't know what I am going to do with. A hopeless mess!

The baby turns inside me. I grab a fistful of hair and tug hard, feeling my scalp lift away from my skull. Why have I let so much time pass? Now, since I gave the cop all my money, I can't even pay for a termination. If I have the baby, Ma will want to take care of it. But if it's a girl, Yong will sell it. And sell me too? It sounds too unbelievable. But Yong's own brother doesn't think so. I remember his face when he talked about Yong. He seemed as sad as Luli whenever she talked about her granddad.

I still have my cell phone. I pull it out from deep in my coat pocket. Over the past few months, I've slowly stopped checking it every moment. The calls and texts from my friends, all unanswered, have gradually trickled off. I only use it to stay in touch with Yong now, and I don't even hear from him that much. I scroll through the other numbers. Zhenzhen, Hong, Ming, other friends who seem like strangers now. My thumb hovers over Luli's number. But there'd be no point in calling her now. She'll be at work. Besides, I have no idea how to explain why I disappeared without warning and ignored her messages for months.

My belly tightens, cramping all the way around my back. I gasp, and my breath catches in my chest. The pain is very real this time.

CHAPTER 15

Luli

In the middle of the night, I'm roused by a low buzz. At first I think it's the alarm, but suddenly I realize it's my phone. I pull it out from under my pillow and fumble it open, wondering who's calling me this time of night.

"Luli?" The voice is muffled. I can hardly hear it.

"Yes?"

"Luli, it's Yun."

"Yun!" I yelp and bolt upright in bed. One of my roommates groans. I lower my voice. "Where are you? Are you okay?"

"I'm at the—" She seems to be whispering. I can't make out what she is saying.

"Yun, I can't hear you. Speak up."

She raises her voice a bit. "I can't talk. I'm at the Institute. Will you come here?"

"At the Institute!" Even though I went looking for her there several months ago, I'm astonished to hear that she's there now. "What are you—"

"I have to go! Come as soon as you can. Tomorrow. Please!"

She clicks off and I'm left wondering how she ended up back at the orphanage. Surely she's not working there? What happened with Yong—with the baby? I try to count the months, but I don't know exactly when Yun got pregnant, so I can't be sure when she would've been due. For the rest of the night, I hardly sleep at all.

The next morning, for the first time since I started at the factory eight months ago, I don't show up for work. Instead, I get on the earliest bus.

As I get off and walk toward the Institute, sleet and wind spitting in my face, my mind circles with questions. Has Yun gotten rid of the baby and asked for a job here? Or did she have it and bring it here to give it away? But that doesn't make sense. People leave their unwanted babies on the street or someplace where they'll be found, too ashamed to bring them to the Institute in person.

"What's this?" The gatekeeper opens the door and pokes his head out of his guardbox. "More visits from old friends?"

"What do you mean?" I mumble, a little surprised he recognizes me.

He comes out and slams the door behind him. "Yesterday we had a young lady like you curled up in front of the gate here." He gestures at the ground. "Only she was like this." He puts his hands in front of his stomach, traces out a big mound, and frowns disapprovingly. "Turns out it was one of you girls who went out a couple of years ago."

Yun. So she *is* still pregnant. "Where is she? Is she okay?"

"She wouldn't talk to anyone." He pulls open the gate to let me in. "I don't know how she got here. Didn't see anyone drop her off, didn't see her walk up. Don't know how long she was there before I noticed her. She was just huddled up there. Wouldn't answer me. I got the director, and as they were getting her inside, one of the caretakers recognized her."

"Is she still here?" I turn toward the looming block of the orphanage.

"The police came. I heard she didn't talk to them either. They sent her over to the other building." He juts his chin toward the building for disabled adults, a twin to the orphanage. "I guess they deemed her mentally deficient."

I nod slowly, though I don't know why. She can't be mentally disabled. I know she isn't. I move toward the building, gazing at three rows of windows, dirty but as orderly as a factory. On the second floor, two figures stand at one of windows, looking down into the courtyard. One of them puts outstretched hands up to the glass and waves at me wildly. I squint and shift, trying to see past the white glare of the winter sky on the glass.

Yun. She's waiting for me. She begins pointing and gesturing. She wants me to go to the back of the building.

I go past the double glass-fronted doors with my head dipped, hoping no one sees me, and hurry around. Just as I come to the back door, it swings open, and Guo is standing there.

"Guo!" I smile, and he grins, his wide-set eyes pinching at the corners. I realize I've rarely seen his open-mouth smile. He's clearly glad to see me, and I'm glad to see him. Although he never talked much, he often trailed Yun and me around the Institute. I suddenly feel bad that I haven't visited him here.

I slip inside and pull the door shut behind me. "It's been a long time. How are you?"

He only bounces his head, though the smile stays plastered on his face.

"Do they treat you well?"

"The same." His voice comes out in a croak. Again I realize how little I knew him. He was like a shadow to us.

"Did Yun send you to get me?"

He nods, and I follow him up the stairs. Inside, the building seems the same as the orphanage. Dim, white-tiled halls, lit only from the open doors of some of the rooms. The fluorescent lights aren't turned on, and the floors and wall tiles are grimy. I peer into the rooms as we go down the hall. Old men and women sit watching small televisions or staring off into space. Some who can walk are pacing. Most of them wear mismatched old clothing, though many have on light-blue Institute-issued shirts.

Everything is dirty, much worse than the orphanage building, and the halls smell terrible, like a toilet. At least the orphanage often had the smell of bleach and cleanser. They keep it up for when potential parents come by. Here, I'm sure visitors are rare. And I don't see any staff.

Guo stops at a room filled with rows of narrow metal beds with thin mattresses. Several women curl under blankets in the cold room. He points to a bed behind the door but doesn't follow when I go in.

Yun is sitting on the side of a bed, her stomach sticking out in front of her like she has a large ball under her coat.

Her eyes light up when she sees me. "You're here!" She gets up clumsily. "I knew you would come!"

I rush over to her and clutch her arms. "Don't get up!" I help her ease herself back down on the bed. I kneel in front of her and keep hold of her arms—studying her face, her pocks, her reddened skin, wind-burned but healthy. She is well. I thought I'd lost her, but she is well, and she still has the baby inside her. I feel tears welling up. I cover my face and sob.

Yun starts patting my hair. "Why are you crying?"

I start laughing—laughing and crying both. She never

did understand people. She just looks at me, puzzled and slightly irritated.

I swipe at my snotty nose with my sleeve. "Where have you been? Were you really in the country? With Yong's ma?"

She nods curtly.

"Why didn't you tell me where you were going?"

"Don't know." She reaches up and begins to pull on a lock of her hair. It's much longer now. "Everything just happened." I take her hand and move it away from her hair, remembering her terrible habit of pulling out strands whenever she was nervous or sad. If it got too bad, the caretakers shaved her head. "Did Yong kidnap you?"

She shakes her head. "Not like that. He took me there so his ma could take care of me. Then he left, wasn't even there."

"But you never answered any of my calls! Or texted me . . ."

"I know. At first it was just that I didn't want to talk about what was happening, or even think about it. I just wanted to ignore everything. I was so sick. I couldn't do anything. Then so much time passed and I still hadn't done anything. I didn't know how I could see anyone like this . . . how I could explain myself. And once I got to the country it was like I was hypnotized. Ma treated me so nicely. She cooked such good things for me, fed me all the time, made me rest. She did everything for me."

There's a tender quality to her tone that I've never heard. I realize she must've liked it there, must've liked Yong's ma. "So what made you leave?"

She looks away from me. "You were right about Yong."

I pull in my lip. "You mean about bride trafficking?" I whisper, glancing behind me at the other women in the ward, but no one is paying any attention to us.

She gives another short nod. "He's in jail now. But Ma and his brother are going to get him out." Her eyes meet mine again. "If the baby's a boy, they'll want to keep it. If it's a girl, his brother says Yong will sell it on the black market."

Sell a baby! What kind of world is this? Though at the same time I wonder why I'm surprised. We saw so many babies as good as thrown away here at the Institute. I suppose if their parents could've gotten rid of them and made some money, they would've done it.

"And he might try to sell me too," Yun adds.

Now I feel as if I've been punched in the stomach. "What? We have to go to the police! Won't they—"

"I don't want to worry about all that now. Once I was out of Yellow Grain Village, it's like I got my senses back. I need your help. I have to get an abortion, but I don't have any money left."

I struggle to keep up with what she's saying. "But isn't it too late for an abortion?" She's so big, she looks as if the baby is about to come out any minute.

"I don't think so. The caretakers talked about it yesterday when I got here. But the Institute doesn't want to pay the medical fees. They decided I'll have the baby here, and they'll put it up for adoption. They can make money on the donation from the parent who adopts the baby."

"What did you say about that?"

"Nothing. I pretended I was mentally disabled so they would take me in. I didn't have anywhere else to go. I was having pains on the bus and thought the baby was going to come out any minute. But they've stopped. And I can't stay here! I waited sixteen years to leave this place! I just want everything to go back like it was before any of this happened—working, being on our own. What if they try to make me a permanent ward? I can't stay here another day!"

I think about how she helped me come to the factory, let me stay in her dorm that first night. Could I get her into my dorm, hide her there? She's so large now, I know she'll attract attention. And what will my dorm mates say?

"Do you have money?" Yun asks. "Remember, they said it'll cost at least 450 yuan."

I nod reluctantly. It isn't that I care about the money. I'm glad I've saved up enough to help her, but I'm scared for her. It doesn't seem safe to have an abortion so late in her pregnancy. What if something goes wrong? I begin to tremble.

"Don't look like that," Yun says impatiently. "I don't know why you want me to have the baby. From the first minute I told you I was pregnant, you wanted me to keep it. After all the time at the Institute. All those foundlings. Didn't that spoil you for babies?"

"But those were babies no one wanted. Sick ones, sad ones, ones with no hope. Our baby wouldn't be like that!"

She presses her lips together. "*Our* baby?"

"Yes! We'll figure something out." I take hold of her hands and squeeze them. "I'll help you take care of it!"

She shakes her head, bewildered. "Luli, why would you want to do that?"

"Because I want to help you. We've grown up together. We're like sisters."

She swallows. "But I don't want a baby," she says softly. She speaks with absolute calm. "I may know how to feed them and wash them and put clothes on them, but I don't really know how to raise one. I want to go back to work, I want to have my own life." A small smile eases into her expression. "Remember how simple it was? Just taking care of ourselves?"

Her eyes sweep across the room to the window, over the beds full of smelly sheets and the rumpled heaps of the wards. The sleet has turned to heavy, wet snow. Just looking at it chills me to the bone. I shiver, dreading going back out there. To me, it looks cold, wet, and miserable, but it's obvious that Yun sees something very different.

CHAPTER 16

Yun

The good thing about the adult unit of the Institute is that there's hardly any staff. At least that's the way it is on this floor where the wards are silent and harmless. It's like they're locked inside their heads.

Luli and I slip through the halls and head downstairs, following Guo. When we get to the back door, Luli hesitates. There's a rough moment when she looks at Guo. He isn't grinning like he was yesterday, when they carried me in and we saw each other. Even though I was acting like I was mentally disabled, I peeked open one eye and raised my eyebrows at him. His blank face cracked open like a melon on display at the market. Now he looks dumb again. So much like the foundlings at the Institute, standing in their cribs, waiting for their food. I know he has Down syndrome, but he isn't as slow-witted as the Institute staff think. Still, we have to leave him behind. We can't do anything for him.

"Guo, we'll visit you again," Luli says. Her voice quavers.

He beams. "And bring the baby with you!"

I flinch but don't say anything.

Luli and I leave, going out into the wet snow. I take a deep breath. The air smells like metal, like coal and exhaust. With a burst of energy, I speed toward the gate as fast as I can with my heavy belly. I pound on the window in the little door of the guardbox. "Let us out!"

The watchman is startled. I laugh at the expression on his face as he opens it.

"What's this?" he says, glancing at the swell of my belly. "You've been released?"

"This isn't a jail! I wasn't arrested. I needed social welfare, but not anymore. My *family* came for me." I nudge Luli with my elbow. Her face is a swirling hotpot of fear, amazement, and giddiness. It makes me want to laugh some more.

"I'd better check with the director." He reaches for the phone.

"Doesn't matter. I'm not a registered ward here!" I stamp over to the gate, feeling the baby turn inside me. Now seems like a good moment to use my trick. I clutch my belly and gasp, faking pain.

Luli cries out. She has an expression of utter horror.

"She's taking me to the hospital!" I tell the guard. I motion fiercely to Luli, willing her to snap out of her shock. She rushes over. I put one arm around her neck, and we hobble to the nearest big avenue and get a taxi.

◆◆◆

We have to stop by the factory so Luli can get her money. I wait in the taxi and watch her cross the empty plaza. The snow is more water than fluff, melting when it hits the concrete, the slick places mirroring the white of the sky. I try not to think about what's going to happen. The other time we went to the clinic, they mentioned pills, cramping, bleeding.

I try to push that out of my mind and gaze at the factory complex on the other side of the gates. Everyone is inside working now. I can see myself in there, bent over my adapter cords and black twist-ties, watching the clock, stiff-necked. I know I won't be working at this factory, but I hope to be working somewhere soon.

Luli returns, worry written on her face. I give the driver the address of the Modern Women's Health Clinic.

"I'll pay you back as soon as I find a position and get my first pay," I say to Luli.

She waves aside my promise. "Yun, I don't think this is a good idea. The baby is so big. Are you sure terminating now will be"—she presses her lips together for a moment and glances at my stomach—"safe?"

I turn away from her and stare out the wet-streaked window. I don't know. I don't want to think about it.

The snow has turned to sleet again. It makes a faint *pizzle* against the glass that I can hear between the *tharummph*, *tharummph* of the windshield wipers. The colors of the signs and lights of the stores glow brightly amid the silvery-gray rain. Funny how just a short time ago I was feeling so happy, free. But now, I'm as low as anyone can be. Trapped, scared.

At the clinic, we eventually get shuttled to the doctors' office and meet with the same one I saw all those months ago, though she doesn't seem to remember me. I lean forward and mutter what I need so the other doctor in the office and his patient can't hear. My doctor gives me a look as if she's been struck by lightning. For a full minute she doesn't say anything.

"You waited a long time. That wasn't wise, you know. I'm surprised the Family Planning Council didn't catch up with you months ago. Sometimes Family Planning forces women to have late-term abortions, but we're not equipped to terminate a pregnancy this far along. And it's highly unlikely a hospital would do it either."

I'm really scared now. There's all kinds of chaos inside of me. The doctor must see that I've started to tremble, but she just says matter-of-factly, "You shouldn't have waited so long. You'll have to pay the social maintenance fee so you can get the birth permit. It will cost you a lot. Around 40,000 yuan."

A hopeless amount. More than I'd earn at a factory job in five years.

Luli stands up. "Thank you," she says meekly to the doctor. Pulling on my arm, she says, "Come on, let's get out of here. Don't worry, it'll be all right. I'll help you."

I let myself be led out.

CHAPTER 17

Luli

We go to the restaurant next door to the clinic. There are only a few other people there, and the television is off. I can hear music playing from a radio in the kitchen. Over a steaming bowl of noodle soup, Yun stares out the window at the pool tables across the street. They're covered in plastic tarps, sleet and snow lightly piling up in the dips. There's no one out there now. I remember the first time I came here, watching Yun outside with Yong, her eyes burning so brightly. Usually she's in quick movement, tossing her hair, smiling, laughing, talking. Now, her face is soft, relaxed, her head turned so I can just see the four pocks that draw everyone's attention. Points of the star, like Granddad's constellation.

"Eat something." I tap her bowl with my chopstick.

She gives me a weak smile but goes back to looking out at the sleet.

"I thought it might be Ming's baby." The words pop out of my mouth. I instantly wish I hadn't said anything.

Yun shrugs. "Might be."

I'm stunned speechless. I bow my head over my soup, stare at the bean threads swimming in the broth. I don't know what to feel. All this time, I haven't been able to decide about Ming.

I hoped that he was over Yun, that everything between them had ended when Yun started seeing Yong.

Well, I won't let it bother me. I'm glad I know now. I stir my noodles and try to eat. Yun is my friend, and I'm glad I've found her. And there's this baby.

"Maybe he could help us," I say. "You could get married. Maybe his parents would take you both in. They could help you pay the fines."

She gives a confused look. "Isn't Ming *your* boyfriend now?"

I put my chopsticks down and shake my head, trying not to show how the question stings.

"We can wait for Yong to get out of jail," Yun says. "I can have the baby, and he can find someone to take it. His brother says there are people who'll pay, even for a girl." The agitated lines are back between her eyebrows, a hard glitter in her eyes. "He can even sell *me* to some farmer, and then I'll run away. I'll make him give me half the money!"

I draw back, shocked. "You would sell a baby? Sell yourself? And trust Yong to give you part of his payment?"

The fire goes out of Yun's eyes. She pushes away her bowl, hot soup sloshing over the edge. "Utterly screwed!" She folds her arms on the table and drops her head on them. I can see now that she doesn't really trust him. That she isn't seriously considering what she said. I lift a hank of her hair off the soup-soaked table and try to pat it dry with one of my gloves.

"Tell me what you remember about your granddad," Yun says, her head still down on the table.

"What?" I'm not sure I heard her right.

She raises her head. "Your granddad. Before he got sick, I mean. What was it like living with him? What was it like where you came from? Your home."

I stir my soup. It's been a long time. And at the Institute it was easier to forget the past than to hang on to it.

I take a deep breath. "In the morning before I went to school, I remember trailing him around the fields and helping him take care of the animals. Near dinnertime he would go out into the field and dig up the sweet potatoes we were going to eat." A fleeting memory of Grandma chopping the potatoes comes back to me. My mouth trembles. I can hardly remember her at all. She died when I was very little. My parents I never knew at all.

Yun says, "When I was with Yong's ma and I saw old men in the village or out in the fields, I thought about you and your granddad. I knew you liked it out in the countryside."

I nod, though the countryside seems distant to me now. Long dead, like Granddad and Grandma. I'm a worker now. I wince, remembering that I'm missing my shift. I hope I won't be fired.

"I don't want to marry some farmer," Yun goes on. "I don't want Yong. Or Ming. Or this baby. I know you think I should want it and take care of it because I was given away, but I don't think I can do it. I don't know how to be a mother! Your grand-dad wanted you, and he still couldn't keep you." Her eyes are level and clear. She nods to herself, making her decision. "If the baby's a boy, I'll let Yong's ma raise it. She'll give it a good life. And if it's a girl, I'll have to take it to the Institute. Maybe it will find a home."

I swallow a lump in my throat. I don't want the baby to go to the Institute. But what else is there to do? This really is the only practical plan.

"Let's go back to the factory," I say. "You can stay with me for now."

Yun eyes me doubtfully. "You'll get fined if anyone reports us."

"I don't care about that." I give an impatient little shrug. "Besides, the factory's running twenty-four hours to make up for the time it'll have to close for the holiday. Lots of the girls will be working late shifts. And anybody we run into will be too tired to care whether you're supposed to be there."

She doesn't need much convincing at this point.

By the time we head back toward the factory, it's almost time for the shift change. Walking in the sleet, I see the red strips of paper pasted outside the doors of businesses, each with a poetry couplet in gold lettering. The couplets remind me that the Spring Festival is just a week and a half away. Shop windows are stocked with firecrackers, lanterns, fancy packaged gifts, and all kinds of huge tote bags the girls at the factory use to lug stuff to their relatives. Everyone is going home to celebrate the New Year with their families, plotting their travel plans when they aren't being worked overtime.

Near the factory, we hang back in the shadows until the trickle of people going through the gates begins to swell. Then we scuttle up behind a large group. I throw my arm around Yun's shoulders so her big stomach is somewhat hidden by my body, and we pass through with no trouble. Everyone is wearing big coats and scarves, hunkering against the sleet, rushing to their departments. We trudge across the courtyard, into the dormitory building, up the stairs to my hall.

Outside my room, I turn to Yun and put my finger to my lips before unlocking the door and poking my head in. The room is dark except for the light spilling in from the plaza floodlights. Three of my roommates are sleeping. All the other beds are empty. I don't know those girls very well because they work different shifts.

I usher Yun over to my bunk, the bottom one nearest the door. Yun sinks onto it, kicks off her boots, and struggles out of her coat, which is soaking wet. I hang it on the end of the bed while she gets under the blanket—a heavy wool plaid, ugly, but I bought it because it was warm and cheap. Yun throws me a grateful smile, and I remember her own pink comforter and wonder where it is now. She has nothing with her except her too-tight coat.

She settles in to sleep. I decide that I'd better report to work for at least the overtime shift. After that, we'll make a plan.

CHAPTER 18

Yun

The need to pee overcomes me just as I'm about to fall asleep. I try to ignore it, but the baby inside me begins to move around, and I feel a little wetness leak out. I get up, squinting in the dark, and feel around under the bed for Luli's slippers. There are two pairs, one soft and fluffy, the other the cheap black plastic kind old men wear. These, I know, must be Luli's, so I jam them on my feet.

Standing up in the dorm, I feel strange, out of place, exposed because of my big belly. My coat is hanging on the bedpost, so I snatch it up and put it on. The dorms aren't heated, and a pregnant girl will attract more attention than someone wearing a coat to the bathroom.

Luli's room is just next to the toilets, so I make it in without anyone noticing me. I dart into a stall. The light is dim here, but when I pull down my underwear I notice a thick discharge that looks like I sneezed in them. I rub it away with toilet paper and flush it, but my underwear still feels a little damp.

I slip back into Luli's room, take off my coat, and quietly step to the lockers. I know she wouldn't mind if I borrow some underwear. All the lockers have padlocks on them, but sometimes the girls just push them in without spinning the numbers or turning their key. I used to do that all the time. I spot a cheap-looking lock that seems like what Luli would buy and reach up to give it a yank.

"What are you doing?"

I spin around. One of Luli's roommates on an upper bunk snaps on a light clamped to the metal bedpost. We both blink at the harsh brightness.

"Who are you?" The girl sits bolt upright in her bed, astonished. She looks several years older than me, maybe in her early twenties.

"I'm a friend of Luli's. I was going to borrow some clean clothes." I move toward Luli's bunk. "She said I could wait for her here." I climb into the bed and cover up, trying to ignore the roommate's prying eyes. I want to tell her to stop looking at me, but it's probably best not to get on her bad side since I need to spend the night. If the roommates aren't agreeable, they can report me. "Don't worry about me." I give a tight smile before I snuggle up under the scratchy blanket and turn my face to the wall.

I hear her jump off her bunk and feel her standing next to my bed. I wish she would go away.

"Where's your husband?"

I twist around to look at her, summoning the most tired expression I can make. "I'm just going to sleep for a bit."

"Luli's probably working overtime until ten." She gives no sign of letting up. "How did you get in here anyway?"

"She let me in a little while ago." I wish she would keep her voice down. I don't want the others to wake up.

The roommate puts her hand on her hips. "She shouldn't have done that!" Her voice is sharp now, and I sit up and shush her.

"What is it?" One of the other roommates rolls over in her bunk, a lower one near the window, and pulls off a red satin sleep mask.

"Luli let her friend in while we were sleeping." She doesn't lower her voice. "She wants to wait here until Luli comes off overtime."

The third girl is awake now too. Although I can't see her on the other side of the fabric someone has hung between the beds for privacy, I feel the bed shift since the bunks are connected head to foot.

"But we have to leave for our shift in a little while." The girl near the window swings her feet off and begins to smooth her mussed hair, which is bleached brown.

"Yes, and there won't be anyone here except for you," the older girl says.

The other two girls come to stand over me. The one I haven't been able to see is clutching an oversized stuffed Hello Kitty. "You can't stay here. We don't know you."

"Don't worry. I'm just going to sleep. Luli will be back in a few hours."

The girls exchange looks.

The one with Hello Kitty frowns at me. "Why don't you go home?"

I shake my head vaguely. "I used to work at this factory. Don't worry about your stuff. I won't take anything."

"She's pregnant," the older girl points out, causing the others to take in my middle. "Better go home to your husband," she says to me.

The long-haired girl gets a sly look. "Maybe she's not married."

This is unbearable. I throw the blankets off and sit up. The girls gawk as if I'm the five-legged ox at the zoo. I hunch over my stomach and pull on my boots. I stand up, yank my coat off the bedpost, and leave the room, slamming the door hard behind me.

For a moment I just stand outside the door, clutching my coat, not knowing what to do next. The hall is dim and quiet, but I know in just a little while the girls who work the second shift will be coming out of their rooms to get ready.

The bathroom.

It's only a few steps away. I duck inside. Two girls are at the sinks, but they don't notice me. I dart into the closest stall, shut the door, and lock it. Standing over the squat toilet, I lean against the tile wall. I can feel its chill through my sweater, so I put on my coat. The scent of cleanser doesn't cover the familiar smell of waste and dirty laundry that is always in the bathrooms. I try to just breathe through my mouth.

The girls at the sink are talking about their Spring Festival plans. The factory will be closing in five days. If all of Luli's roommates go home for the holidays, then we'll have two weeks of peace and quiet to figure something out. For now, I'll just wait here until her shift is over.

CHAPTER 19

Luli

When I arrive at the workroom, I tell Foreman Chen that I've been sick but that I don't want to miss the overtime now that I feel better. He frowns but accepts the story with a grunt and motions me toward an empty station. I walk toward it, keeping my head down, though out of the corner of my eye I can see Ming, watching me from across the room.

Several times during my shift, he pushes his cart by me and throws me questioning looks. I'm sure he is wondering where I have been all day. I try to keep my eyes averted from him.

I wonder what Ming and his father would think if they knew Yun might be carrying Ming's baby. I work faster. I can't think about that now. It doesn't matter whose baby it is. As far as I'm concerned, the baby belongs to Yun and me, even if Yun doesn't want it.

I am so glad she is back.

As I settle into my automatic mode, though, my thoughts spin dangerously fast. She's so big! Does she know when the baby's coming? She can stay in my room through the holidays, if my roommates agree. They'll all be leaving for home soon. But then what? We'll have to find her a room. Find some way to cover the hospital costs.

A boy will go to Yong's mother. A girl will go to the Institute. The thought of that makes my hands tremble. I remember what Yun said about giving the baby to Yong for private adoption, herself being sold as a wife. But I know she only said that because she's worried about money. I'll take care of her until she can find a position.

I glance up at the clock. I didn't like leaving her back at the dorm. I have a bad feeling.

CHAPTER 20

Yun

A long time passes while I'm in the stall. Girls move in and out of the bathroom, sometimes tapping on the door, but moving on when I say I'm going to be awhile. No one seems to notice that I don't come out. The bathroom quiets. I guess the late shifts have started and the girls who work during the day are still on overtime.

The pulling pressure in my lower belly and between my legs becomes so heavy that I have to sit, squeezed awkwardly to one side of the squat toilet. I can't put my legs together, so I have to lean back with one foot propped up on the stall door and the other straddled across the squat to the opposite corner. My coat is tucked up so the hem won't fall into the long shallow toilet bowl. It isn't long before I have to stand up again because the position begins to strain my back in a different way. As I'm struggling to my feet, a hard cramp doubles me over. Worse than any monthly cramp I ever had, worse than the cramps I had on the bus yesterday. I gasp, then hold my breath.

The cramp eases off. I pant to get my breath, shaking and cold-sweating in my coat. I feel clammy in my armpits and back and between my legs where my underwear is still damp. I hate how scared I feel.

Nothing happens for a long while. My panic dies down a little. I decide to see if I can get back into Luli's room. If only I can stretch out and rest. The few cramps I had yesterday went away once I was resting at the Institute.

I peer out of my stall—the bathroom is empty. Out in the hall—also empty. Luli's door—locked.

The thought of going back to the toilet suffocates me. I have a sudden urge to just leave the dorm entirely. It's snowing or raining outside—cold, I'm sure—but I can see myself out there breathing, going somewhere.

But where would I go?

My belly and backside suddenly tighten again, shooting pain all around my middle. I grip the door handle of Luli's room and nearly cry out, but my voice is caught in my throat. The pain paralyzes me. When it's over, my legs feel as if they'll collapse. I steady myself against the wall and lurch back to the bathroom.

I consider the stalls, but the thought of being folded in there again is unbearable. So I go to the far side of the bathroom near the high frosted window, take off my coat, and lay it on the floor in the corner. I crawl onto it, roll onto my side, and wait.

I have two more cramps before I have to admit something is happening. The pressure between my legs hasn't eased up since I lay down. In fact, the feeling has increased.

I pull out my phone—and curse, realizing Luli won't be able to answer her phone at work.

I scroll through the numbers. Everyone would be at work now except Yong. He's probably still in jail, unless Wei has gotten him out already. I bring up his number. My thumb hangs over the call button.

Another cramp. I drop the phone, clutching my belly and groaning. They're coming more often now.

When it stops, I pick up my phone and check the time. It's almost 8:30. Another hour and a half and Luli will be back. I clamp my thighs together. I'm sure I can hold the baby inside until then.

CHAPTER 21

Luli

As soon as the late shift bell rings, I hop off my seat and run out the door while everyone else is still stretching and pushing their stools under the worktables. In the corridor, I hear someone calling me. I turn and see Ming. He grins and waves for me to wait, but I spin around and bolt away. I glance back and see him standing there, confused, workers streaming out of the workroom around him.

I rush back to the dormitory.

Just inside the building, Yuling, who lives on my floor, sees me and streaks toward me, shouting my name. I don't even ask; I know something has happened with Yun. I follow Yuling up the stairs and along the hall, which is still mostly deserted. I slow as we get close to my room, but Yuling grabs my hand and pulls me to the bathroom.

Yun is on the floor in the far corner, panting like an animal. Her eyes are squeezed closed and her face is twisted in pain, the fluorescent lights over the mirrors giving her skin a greenish cast.

"I came in, and she was calling for you," Yuling says. "Yelled at me to go get you."

I dash over to Yun and kneel beside her. She opens her eyes

and grabs my hand, squeezing so hard it's like she's crushing my bones. I let her. Seeing her in so much agony makes my chest hurt.

After a moment, Yun's grip loosens on me. Her face is slick with sweat, but the rigid look falls away. "You're here." She breathes the words so faintly between pants, I almost don't hear.

Yuling crouches behind me. "Is she having a baby?"

I nod, fighting down my own panic.

"She has to go to the hospital!" Yuling says.

"Yes. Help me get her up!"

We lift her, and she slings her arms around our shoulders. We half-drag her out of the bathroom, but as soon as we reach the hallway Yun stops. She grabs her sides, clenched in pain again.

I peer down the long hall toward the stairs at the other end. I have no idea how we're going to get there and then down four flights. And then across the complex to the front gates. And then to the hospital. I have plenty of money for a taxi, but the closest hospital is—

I can hear hollow voices and the clomp of footsteps in the stairwell, girls arriving back from work. "Into my room! Right there!" I fumble for my keys and thrust them at Yuling. She unlocks the door and pushes it open. I get Yun inside and lower her onto my bunk while Yuling clicks on the overhead light.

I drop to sit on the edge of the bunk to catch my breath.

"It's coming! I know it is!" Yun huffs. She starts twisting side to side on the bed. For a moment, I think she's writhing in agony. But no—she's just trying to wriggle off her pants. I reach over to help her tug them off.

"She can't have a baby here!" Yuling pulls her phone from a pocket. "I'm going to call an ambulance!"

"No!" Yun growls fiercely.

Startled, Yuling freezes. We look at each other, not knowing what to do. I turn back to Yun.

"No. The fines . . . the hospital charges . . ." She's lying back with her knees up, her eyes closed, a moment of rest. I'm petrified, knowing another terrible pain is coming.

Yuling is right—we need an ambulance, Yun needs to get to a hospital. But I don't have anywhere near 40,000 yuan. What if we get all the way there, only to be turned away because we can't pay for the birth permit?

"Yun," I say, "what should we—"

Yun lets out another smothered cry. Her fingers scrunch up the blanket she's lying on.

The baby is coming. Right now. Even if Yun would agree to try the hospital, I'm not sure we'd make it there in time.

I turn to Yuling desperately. "Do you know anyone on this floor who has children?" I know lots of women come from the countryside to work in the factories, leaving their children with grandparents, sending money home for their education. Most of them live off grounds with their husbands, though surely *someone* in this dorm has had a child and would know how to help deliver one.

Suddenly I think of Dali. She came from the countryside, and she has a much younger brother she helps support. She's the smartest person I know. "Upstairs! Room 606! Get Dali!"

Yuling races out of the room. I joggle my leg nervously, biting at my hangnails as I watch Yun. She keeps her eyes closed, the skin between her brows pinched up like she's concentrating on something. I want to say something that will help her, but I can't think of anything. I can't believe this is happening. I've never been so scared.

Yun has two more pains before the door flies open and Yuling is back. Dali is with her. I jump up, relieved.

"Oh, shit!" Dali says when she sees Yun lying in the bed, naked from the waist down. "Move over, move over. I know what to do."

I scramble out of the way, and Dali crouches next to the bed. "I helped my mother when she had my little brother." She yanks my blanket off the foot of the bed where Yun has kicked it, folds it into a pad, and places it on the floor. "Yun, get up! Get on your knees and lean over the bed."

Yun rolls her eyes to Dali and blinks, but when she doesn't move, Dali slips her arm under her shoulders and hoists her up until she starts getting off the bed. She kneels at the side of it with my pillow folded and tucked under her arms. Her naked bottom shines pale and white. Although it's astonishing to see her like this, I can't help thinking that from behind I can hardly tell she's pregnant. How did all this happen?

Yuling has left the door open, and several girls pass by on the way to the bathroom. They see what's happening and begin crowding behind her. I gesture furiously at Yuling, and she quickly shuts the door.

I curse under my breath, but then Yun is having another cramp. She grits her teeth, her face screaming pain, but no sound comes out except heaves of breath. I don't know how she isn't yelling. I bite on my own knuckle to keep from crying out.

There's knocking on the door. Someone shouts, "What's going on?"

I hear the key turn, and the door starts to open.

I push Yuling out of the way, lunge to the door, and shove it closed. I jam my foot against it.

Pounding starts from the other side. "Who's in there? Luli? It's Shu! You can't keep me out!"

A roommate. Most of them are getting off the overtime shift. They'll all be here soon. They have to sleep. If I don't let them in, they'll report me. I look at Yuling, but she just gives me a don't-know-what-to-do face.

"Wait a minute." Dali wiggles off her coat and puts it over Yun's naked backside. She gestures at me to go ahead.

I crack open the door. There are several girls around Shu. I will myself to speak calmly. "It's my friend. She's sick." I gesture for the others to go away. They try to peer in, but I hold the door close and keep myself wedged tightly in the opening.

"Let me in now, " Shu whines. "I'm tired."

I nod at her friends. Shu gets the message and shoos them away. Once they've gone into the bathroom, I let her slip through.

Shu gapes at Dali and Yun bent over the bedside. "What sort of sick?"

I ignore her, but Yuling pipes up, "She's having a baby!"

I shush her, but the door opens and three more of my roommates come in. They're all worn out, and I almost think they would have just gone to their bunks without noticing, except that Shu makes a big show of rushing over to gawk at Yun. The other girls are instantly curious. All their tiredness falls away as they circle around with questions and probing eyes.

"Be quiet!" Dali snaps at them. She snatches the coat off Yun. "It's coming. I can see the head!"

The girls gasp, then fall silent. I draw back, putting my cold hands to my cheeks.

Yun begins to groan, a deep guttural animal sound. She's been so quiet with her pain before now. Brave. I'm sure I'm more scared than she is.

"Get some towels or something!" Dali shouts.

We all scramble to our lockers between the bunks. I'm so nervous I can't get my lock unfastened, and by the time I place my towel on the floor with the others, Yun is squatting, and I can see a dark dome between her legs.

"Luli, get behind her and let her lean on you," Dali orders.

I quickly move into place, unsure of how to position myself. But Yun leans back between my legs and loops her arms around my bent knees as if she does this all the time. I can feel the heat coming off her. The room is hushed except for Yun gasping and moaning as she pushes. Even Dali looks frightened as she holds a towel under the baby, waiting for it to come out.

Yun groans, nearly a roar, and now the baby's head is fully out—now a shoulder. "Pull it!" she rasps.

"You have to push it out!" Dali's hands tremble as she moves the towel closer to the baby.

Yun takes several breaths. Her hair is matted to her flushed, damp face. Beads of sweat spring up at her temples, and she leaks tears. I grab one of the towels the girls have thrown on the bed and mop her face.

"You can do it. You can do it." I lean forward to put my face next to hers and whisper in her ear, feeling tears running down my own cheeks. "It's almost out. You're almost done!"

Her arms clamp hard against my legs. Her jaw clenches, and she pushes with a hard, low moan. I feel her whole body shudder, and she releases a deep, shaky sigh. Then Dali has the baby in a towel.

CHAPTER 22

Yun

I'm so tired I just want to lie down and sleep. Too exhausted to speak, I weakly nudge against Luli, trying to get her to move so I can stretch out. She understands without needing me to say anything. Gently, she unfolds her knees from under my arms where she's been propping me up, then scoots back. The baby is crying, a high-pitched, jagged, unreal noise. Around me, the girls are squealing and gushing over it, but they rush to spread blankets out on the cool cement floor before I lie back. I don't care about the blankets. I just want to rest. I close my eyes against the glaring fluorescent tube overhead, listening to the thrilled and horrified voices of the girls.

"It's so cute!"

"And so tiny!"

"Is it okay? What's all that white stuff?"

"Is it a girl or a boy?"

"Girl!" Dali announces.

The clamor in the room swells as the girls get excited again. Girl or boy, it doesn't matter to me. My body feels deflated, drained, but I can still feel some cramping in my belly.

Dali barks above the noise, "Somebody! Yuling, go to my room and get my laptop!"

I open my eyes and see her squatting beside me, rubbing the baby in the towel on the floor.

"Take my keys." She thrusts her chin upward at Yuling to show the key hanging on a lanyard around her neck. "It's in my locker. The top one with my family's photo."

Yuling reaches over and lifts the lanyard from around Dali's neck.

Luli, sitting on her heels beside me, asks Dali, "Why do you need your computer?" Her voice is shaky, nervous, but her eyes are on the baby, full of wonder.

"Who has scissors? We have to cut the cord. I also need some strips of cloth or string," Dali says.

Two of the girls go to search their lockers before Dali answers Luli. "There's more to do. I want to check on the internet to make sure we're doing everything right. I was twelve when my brother was born." She smiles down at the baby. "I helped my grandma bring him out at home, but that was a long time ago. Eight years. I'm a little rusty."

Luli swallows. "When you say there's more to do . . ." She trails off.

Dali answers the unfinished question. "After we cut the cord, something else has to come out, or else she"—she thrusts her chin at me this time—"can get very sick."

I curl up against the cramps as the scissors are found, the computer arrives. Dali orders someone to get out a hot plate and sterilize the scissors. It all happens around me like I'm not a part of it. I feel as if I'm not there, only half conscious of some hazy scene.

The cord is finally cut and tied off. Dali gives the baby to Luli. It's still crying, the noise like the alley cats in Yellow Grain Village. Has it only been two days since I was there? By now, Ma surely knows I've left the jail. She's probably panicked. I have a twinge of guilt about that.

Luli bounces the baby as she paces and murmurs to her anxiously. I just want to drift off, but I do everything that Dali tells me to do to "push out the placenta." The other girls smother their horror at what comes out. Even Dali makes a face as she folds it up into a towel with stiff arms and snaps at someone to find a plastic bag.

The girls stay up, all excited, helpful, nice. They rush around to help, cleaning up the mess, searching for pads and spare cloth to use as makeshift diapers, taking turns holding the baby until she calms, trying out names. They act like this is a party, and the baby is the center of it. I'm outside all the commotion. Like falling asleep watching a program on television.

It seems like a long time before Luli helps me up into her bunk. I feel so weak, as if my shuddering legs won't hold me up.

When I'm finally settled under someone's purple comforter, the girls clean up the floor. Luli sits on the edge of the bed and holds the baby out to me. I don't want to take her, but Luli presses her on me.

I've held little babies before at the Institute. Picked them up to change them, washed them, but never held them just to hold. There were too many of them. Of us.

"I don't think we've ever seen one this new before," I say. She's pink-white and so tiny wrapped in the towel, she reminds me of a newborn mouse. She's not bawling her lungs out anymore, just making weak little sounds as she twists in my arms.

Luli tears her watery eyes away from the baby and glances at me. Her smile pulls wider for a moment before she goes back to gazing at the baby. A faint smile stays on her face, that soft look. "Isn't she amazing? I can't believe it. And you! You were so strong!" She blinks several times until a wet track comes down her cheek. "It must've hurt so much. I could see it did. But look! Look at her."

I glance down at the baby again. They all think she's so cute, but all I see is a splotchy, squished face that's puffed around the eyes. "She looks so strange." I murmur, feeling distant and strange myself. I don't feel the same about her as Luli does. I wonder why.

Almost as if she's heard my thoughts, Luli says, "You're tired. You need to rest." She takes the baby from me and starts to get up, but a thin arm shoots out of the towel and the baby jerks awake. She starts crying again, short little bleats.

The nervous look springs back into Luli's face. She calls to Dali, who's sitting on the bunk across from us reading on her laptop.

"She's probably hungry." Dali puts her laptop down and comes over. "You'll have to feed her," she tells me matter-of-factly. "I'll try to help you get started. It can be hard getting her to latch onto the breast." She takes the baby from Luli and sits next to me.

I sigh. I really am so very tired, but I do as she says.

CHAPTER 23

Luli

My roommates drop off to sleep between two and three in the morning. Squeezed in with Yun and the baby on my bunk, I only catch a few snatches of sleep all night. Yun hardly moves. But she does snore deeply and loudly, disturbing the baby on her other side, who wriggles and twitches in her towel and makes strange snorts and shuddering pants that have me sitting up to squint at her in the darkness. She never fully wakes and seems to settle back down each time, but it takes ages for my own nerves to calm after each startle.

Everyone has a hard time getting up in the morning. An alarm beeps for what seems like forever before Shu shouts for someone to shut it off. The others stumble out of bed at the last minute, cooing at the baby before dragging off to the morning shift. "Make sure Yun drinks plenty of water to keep her milk going," Dali tells me on her way out.

I get dressed, but I don't go to work. I know I'll be fined another 20 yuan, but I can't leave the baby and Yun. She's still weak, and she doesn't know about newborns. Neither do I, really. Still, I can't abandon Yun for all those hours.

Once all the girls have left, Yun hobbles to the toilet, wincing in pain, and I lie down on my side to watch over the baby sleeping on my bunk. I realize she'll need clothes, diapers, pacifiers. What else? I think back to the Institute babies dressed in mismatched clothing and trapped in thick swaddles. They were placed flat on their backs in the line of cribs, staring at the ceiling. Their room always smelled of waste. I pinch up my face at the memory.

The baby's small, round mouth begins moving, her little pink tongue slipping in and out, and her head turning side to side. She's waking up, hungry. I will Yun to hurry back. The baby starts making her little cries. I pull her close to me and pat her nervously.

Yun finally comes back. I sit up, pick up the baby, and hold her out to Yun. "She's hungry."

Yun gingerly climbs back into the bed, leaning against the wall, and lifts her shirt.

I hand the baby to her. "She sounds like a baby goat, don't you think?" I say.

Yun nods, though I'm not sure if she's ever seen any goats. She fumbles with the baby, holding her like a bundle of wet laundry, trying to get her to latch on. "I don't know what I'm doing."

The baby fusses and cries harder, her face turning red.

"I can't get her to do this!" Yun's voice is sharp with frustration. She starts to put the baby aside.

"But you did it last night." I run over to Shu's bed and take her pillow. "Here, lift her up." I push the pillow against Yun and help her put the baby on it. "Remember, you have to turn her toward you. Push your breast into her mouth." I swallow my embarrassment at the word. After all, I've seen Yun half naked, a baby coming out of her.

I wish Dali were here, but I don't say it out loud. We work

at getting the baby to eat. The baby gobbles one second, then thrashes her head around discontentedly. Yun is getting impatient. I'm afraid she will give up, so I keep a smile stretched on my face the best I can, though the baby's crying scares me and pulls at my nerves too.

Finally, the baby seems to settle into the feeding. Yun gives a deep sigh, closes her eyes, and rests her head against the wall.

"I'm going to get some food and drinks for you," I tell her. "And some things for the baby. Clothes, diapers . . ."

Her face pinches up a little. I don't know if it's from what I said or if the baby has hurt her.

"I know!" I say in a rush. "I'll get some formula and a bottle. That should be easier, right? We know how to feed babies from a bottle."

Yun gives a tired little smile and nods once.

The door opens and my other three roommates, the ones who are working the night shift this week, file in. Right away, they see Yun and the baby.

There's a long moment of silence before Hui, who's the oldest in our dorm, turns to me. "What's she doing back here? She had the baby?"

"Last night!" I smile proudly at Yun and the baby. "Shut the door now," I urge the girls. "There's a draft in the hall. I'm glad you're back. I have to go out and buy things for the baby. I didn't want to leave them alone."

Hui closes the door while Jinghua and Liling bend for a better look.

"Why isn't she at the hospital? Where's her husband?" Hui asks.

"She had the baby here," I say. "It was an emergency. It happened so fast."

"Here!" Jinghua and Liling gasp.

I'm actually a bit tickled by the horrified shock on their faces. I try to catch Yun's eye, but she's gazing at the purple blanket around her legs. "All the others helped," I explain. "And Dali from upstairs."

"Really!" Liling slowly shakes her head, amazed.

"What about the father?" Hui asks again. She doesn't smile.

I glance at Yun. Her jaw is set firm. The feeling of delight leaves me. I shake my head at Hui, not sure how much to say.

"Is he coming to get her?"

Yun is still staring down at the blanket, but I'm sure she's been listening to every word, just unwilling to say anything. "No," I answer.

Hui takes that in. She doesn't say anything as she pulls off her coat and throws it on her bed. Liling takes off her coat as well, but as soon as she has it off, she's back at my bunk with Jinghua, fawning over the baby. "I didn't know you were going to have it so soon. We could have called the hospital for you," she says to Yun.

Hui says to me, "What is she going to do now?"

We haven't talked about a plan yet. I look at Hui helplessly for a moment. She's always the strictest one in our room. Telling the girls to turn down their music or move their wet clothes hanging too close to her space. "She just had the baby in the middle of the night. She has to rest before anything else."

"No husband?" she drills. "What about her family?"

"She's like me," I say. "Came out of the orphanage."

Hui looks at Yun, at me, back at Yun as she takes off her work shirt, folds it, and places it in her locker. Gradually the stiffness seems to leave her. When Liling puts her finger in the baby's hand and squeals her delight, Hui even smiles. Relief rushes through me.

"I'm going to go shopping now." I put on my coat and tell Yun that I'll be right back.

Hui, carrying her soap and washcloth, follows me into the hall. "Luli," she says, "what's she going to do?"

I take a deep breath, disappointed and cautious. I thought she had decided to ease up. "We haven't talked about it yet. Everything just happened."

"I don't think this *just happened*." She raises her eyebrows archly. "Did she break up with the father?"

I nod. I don't tell her Yong is in jail. The point is, he isn't going to help her. And I don't want him to.

"She can't stay here, Luli. With a baby! With everyone working so hard—overtime, the night shift. It's fun for the girls right now, but we have to sleep. A crying baby will make us crazy." I have to admit she's not being unreasonable. The girls who have been forced to do the night shift are exhausted— and even crankier than the rest of us, who just have overtime shifts added.

"Besides. The dorm manager is going to find out. You can't keep a baby quiet, and even if our roommates don't say anything, you know the other girls on the hall will find out sooner or later."

I glance nervously down the hall. I wasn't worried about getting in trouble if I got caught sharing my bunk, but trying to keep a baby here would definitely get me fired. Then both of us—all three of us—would be kicked out of here with nowhere else to go. "Don't worry. We'll get it sorted out." I think of Ma. The baby isn't a boy like she expected, but maybe . . .

"Is she thinking about taking it to an orphanage?"

"No!" The word comes out loud and angry.

Hui blinks several times. I instantly regret shouting and peer down the hall to make sure I haven't attracted any attention. I didn't mean to snap, but now that I've seen the baby and held her, I can't bear to think of Yun giving her away.

I lower my voice. "Our break for Spring Festival is just three days away. Everyone will be going home. Just let her stay through the break." I try to speak calmly, but I can hear the pleading in my voice. "She just needs some time to recover. Then we'll . . . take them to the baby's grandma." If we can't think of a better option, we might be able to convince Yong's ma to take the baby even though she isn't a boy. From the way Yun talked about Ma, maybe there's a chance.

"It's not just my decision." Hui's face is still stiff, but my heart jumps because she doesn't refuse. I know the other girls will be fine with it.

"I'll ask the others when they get off their shifts," I promise.

"But how are you going to keep it a secret?" Hui seems genuinely concerned now, not just being strict. "You'll get found out. Then you'll lose your job and be forced to leave before the break is over."

I wish I'd asked the other girls to keep quiet about this. They skipped the morning meal and will work late, but the other meal times and the walk back to the dorm will give them plenty of time to talk.

"Where does the grandma live?" Hui asks. "If you have to travel any distance, you'd better work on getting your tickets. You've never traveled during the Spring Festival, you don't realize how impossible it is."

I duck my head to let her know I understand, but mostly I'm eager to get away.

***

I run to the closest shopping lane and get everything I think Yun and the baby will need from the crammed stalls. A bottle, some formula, a package of diapers that I hope will last at least a few days, a pink blanket with little white dots, a few onesies, and a miniature puffy purple coat. I would have liked to take my time fingering the tiny clothes and picking out just the right outfits for the baby—plus some gifts for Ma, who I am more and more convinced will agree to keep her—but I start to worry about Hui's warning.

For weeks, I've been hearing everyone complain about the Spring Festival travel migration—hours spent at internet cafés trying to buy train or bus tickets in advance. Not having any place to go, I wasn't affected by it. Now, the more I think about it, the more I want to get to the bus station and buy tickets.

I bring the baby things, some fried dough sticks, and some Cokes to the dorm and tell Yun my plan. She doesn't say much—doesn't seem excited or even relieved at the prospect of going back to Yong's ma. But she doesn't protest either. When I ask, she tells me the name of Ma's village again. I set off for the bus station.

I'm there by mid-morning. See well before I reach the plaza outside the station, I can see that it's mobbed. People are shoulder to shoulder in their thick coats, clutching their bags, in a disorderly mess that in no way resembles a line. I join the edge of the crowd, which is nearly overflowing into the street. A police officer comes up and motions with his nightstick for everyone to move forward. I squeeze up onto the curb as the buses screech by.

I strain to see over the heads. The entrance to the station

seems so far away, and from what I glimpse of the wide-open doors, it's crammed full of people. There is nothing to do but wait. The day is the color of smoke, but at least it isn't raining or snowing. Gusts of wind whistle high over the heads of the crowd, swirling up stray plastic bags and paper. I press in tighter, using the people around me to block the blustering cold.

By early afternoon my stomach is rumbling. I can smell food and see steam blowing at the edge of the plaza, though I can't see the carts. I don't want to lose my place in the crowd, but after another hour's gone by, I *have* to have something to eat. I start threading my way to the side of the plaza.

"Hot boiled eggs! Hot boiled eggs! Good and hot!"

I head toward the voice until I come to the middle of the station yard. An old woman stuffed in a thick, padded coat sits on the wide ledge of a concrete planter with a coal stove in front of her. People jostle all around, but they give her stove a small space as she scoops up eggs and hands them out. I wait my turn until she sees me.

"How many?" she asks.

I hold up six fingers and she begins dipping into the pot.

"You going home then?" she says as she drops the eggs into a plastic bag. "Good girl who helps your family?" She twists the bag and holds it out to me.

I smile shyly and duck my head as I dig out my money. She thinks I'm like Dali—working in the city, making the annual trip home. A lucky girl who has her own money and a family she's helping.

I take my eggs and dive back into the throng.

By the time I make it into the building, I've been standing in the cold so long that my hands and face are frozen. My elbows are sore from the poking I've had to do to keep my position as people try to push by me. The station is lit white with fluorescent light, and it's turning dark outside.

At last I make it to the ticket window. I ask the agent, a sharp-looking woman with close-cropped hair, for two tickets to Yellow Grain Village. She punches her keyboard for several moments. "No tickets left to Yellow Grain Village," she says. "Next!"

The man behind me barges forward, pushing me aside. My heart plummets. I waited so long and was dismissed so quickly! In my distress, I almost let myself be swallowed back up by the crowd. But as much as I want to get back to the dorm and check on Yun and the baby, I know I have to get them to Ma's.

I thrust out my elbows and wedge myself in front of the man, even though he is already talking through the hole in the glass. The clerk's mouth forms a little o shape and her eyebrows shoot up beneath the fringe of her bangs. I can hear the man muttering curses behind me.

"But what about anything next week?"

"What town again?"

I raise my voice. "Yellow Grain Village."

She taps at her computer again. "Nothing for three weeks. Everything is already booked through the Spring Festival. After the Festival, everything is open. You want to book?"

I bite my lips, feeling the sharp cut of my teeth. Three weeks is too long to wait. I have to find some way to get to Ma's before everyone gets back from Spring Festival.

CHAPTER 24

Yun

Luli comes back with three hard-boiled eggs for me. Her first breathless words are "How's the baby?"

I grimace, looking at the lumpy infant lying next to me on the bed. "She's crying all the time. I'm so worn out. I don't know how long I can keep doing this."

"Well, of course you're worn out! You've barely had anything to eat all day!" She sits down on the edge of the bunk and peels the eggs, careful to get every bit of shell off the whites, which are no longer white, but stained brown and veined with tea and soy. She hands me the first one, and I bite into it even though I don't want it. It's cold, and the yolk is chalky in my mouth. I take a swig of Coke to get it down. When Luli turns to pick up the baby, I set the Coke can next to the bed and place the other half of the egg on top of it.

"I couldn't get any tickets though," Luli says. "It really was as bad as everyone says." The bright look on her face clouds. "There won't be any trouble getting tickets after Spring Festival, but I wish we could go now. I'm afraid that since I'm skipping work, they'll fire me and make me leave the dorm."

"It's just three more days until the break. Go back to work." As soon as the words are out of my mouth, I start to feel

156

nervous. I don't want to stay by myself with the baby again.

Luli shakes her head. "You need help. You can't take care of her by yourself. How was it today?"

I shrug. I feel a tiredness so deep in my bones I could have completely tuned out the baby's squalling, except that Jinghua and Liling huffed and grumbled and put their pillows over their heads trying to sleep. Despite having fussed over the baby earlier, they clearly weren't interested in pitching in. Hui got up to help me once, but her bleary face showed she wasn't happy to do it. I spent all day pushing a bottle into the baby's mouth, trying to keep it quiet.

If I tell Luli that, she'll feel guilty for leaving me alone. So instead I say, "Your roommates had a hard time trying to sleep, but they were nice enough. They gave me snacks before they left for their shift."

The baby's fussing again. Luli stands up, puts her to her shoulder, and jounces her as if there's nothing more natural. She walks back and forth, patting and humming. The baby doesn't stop crying.

All day with the crying, I thought about the Institute. The babies and little ones, dull and silent most of the time, suddenly wailing around the mealtimes. I remember Luli picking them up sometimes and cuddling them. The first time I saw her do it, I was so puzzled that I asked what she was doing. She looked at me strangely and simply said, "Holding her."

"Do you think she's hungry?" Luli asks now. "Maybe we should feed her."

"I've been feeding her all day!"

Still, Luli gets a bottle and starts feeding her. She gazes down at the baby, her face as fond as I've ever seen it. I wonder if there is something wrong with me that I don't feel like that.

Even if I wanted to keep her, there's no way I could work and take care of a baby. And if I'm not working I'll never pay off the Family Planning fines. Which means the baby won't get a hukou. She won't be able to go to school, or get medical care, or find a decent job when she's old enough. I think of how Yong grew up without a hukou, how his family blames that for everything that's gone wrong in his life. At least in an orphanage, she'd get registered properly.

If I take her to the Institute, would I leave her outside the gatehouse when the gatekeeper isn't looking, or would I just march her in and sign away my right to her? The only thing that stopped me from taking her today is that I'm too weak.

But once she's at the Institute, then what? I'm still in a mess. I can barely sit up right now—it's not as if I can march into the job center and get a new position tomorrow. And Luli's putting her own job at risk every second she keeps me here.

I'm still wondering if Yong can sell the baby for private adoption. It's what he was planning to do all along—I'm sure of that now. The money could carry me over until I get a position.

But I don't see how I can care for her even one more day.

"Maybe you should go ahead and take her to the Institute," I say.

Luli's eyes snap to me, panicked.

"That way I'll be able to get my energy back," I rush on. "And I can go back to work after the Spring Festival. It'll be easy to get a position then."

"Yun, we *can't*. Don't you remember what it was like there?"

"There is nothing wrong with this baby," I remind her, a little impatiently. "She would get a family pretty quickly. And she doesn't feel like mine. I don't even know if I like her."

Luli is horror-stricken. "But she looks like you! Look at her mouth, and how the hair at her forehead comes to a point." She turns the baby toward me.

I look again, but I don't know what Luli is talking about. I only see that the baby has no pocks. "Doesn't seem like mine at all. Isn't that strange? You, and even your roommates, like her more than I do."

"Don't say that!" Luli crouches beside the bed. "Just wait. We'll go to Ma's. You said she wants the baby—I'm sure she won't mind that it's a girl, once she sees her. She'll take care of both of you. And I'll help until you've recovered enough to find work. You're just tired. When you feel better, you'll grow to like the baby. I know you will! After all, you grew to like me eventually."

That makes me smile a little, but I'm still not sure. I suppose something is wrong with me, since I never had a family. Luli is my best friend, but a friend isn't a baby.

"Just give it some time," Luli pleads. "Just do this for me!"

"Do it for *you*?" I snap, a flare of anger coming over me. "I know you say you'll help, but *I'm* the one who had this baby. *I* carried her and had all the pain of her coming out. And because of her, *I* have no job, no money. *I* have to worry about Family Planning coming after me for the fines. Not you. This isn't just some sort of small favor—this is my life and I have to decide what to do!"

Tears shine in Luli's eyes. "I'm sorry, Yun. I just—I just think you'll *both* be better off at Ma's. My roommates won't let you stay here much longer. Ma would make sure you ate right and got plenty of rest so you could get your strength back and be fit for work again. And if you bring the baby, don't you think Ma would be more likely to take you in than if you showed up by yourself?"

She has a point.

And the fact is, I'm depending on Luli for everything right now. I'm not strong enough to walk all the way to the Institute carrying a baby. And if Luli won't lend me the money for a cab to get there or for another place to stay, Ma really is the only alternative, at least for now.

Later I can decide what to do in the long term. Right now, I feel so drained I just don't care. I sigh and nod slowly.

Luli heaves a sigh of relief. "I wish we could go now! I know everything will be fine if we could just get to Ma's." She stares toward the window—dark outside except for the yellow flood-lights. Her face crimps, thinking, planning.

"How about Ming?" I suddenly remember that Ming has an older cousin who owns a car. Once he drove us to Yingze Park, back when we were together. That was such a long time ago. I know that Ming was mad at me when I started up with Yong, but he has Luli now. "I think if you asked him, he would help."

CHAPTER 25

Luli

As I wait for Ming to get off his shift, snow starts to fall. The heavy, wet flakes gleam in the floodlights and drop silently to the concrete of the empty plaza. The bell rings, breaking the quiet, and a few moments later everyone floods out the doors, hunching over to shield themselves from the snow. I stand on my toes, half hidden behind a light post in case Ming's father, Foreman Chen, comes out and notices me, even though it's unlikely that he would know my face from any of the others.

When I spot Ming, I push my way over to him and snag his coat. He turns, irritated, but as soon as he sees me, his expression breaks open. My heart jumps. He's glad to see me.

"I was wondering about you!" Ming says. "Have you been sick again?"

I shake my head. We're surrounded by people. Not a good place to talk. I lead him closer to the building where there's a little more shelter from the snow.

"Why didn't you answer my texts?"

"Yun's had the baby, Ming," I say, ignoring his question. "We have to get her to Yong's mother's house."

A bewildered look crosses his face. "Where is she?"

"She's in my room."

His brows furrow as my words begin to sink in. "Did she just show up?"

I take a deep breath, wondering how much I should explain to him. "She was staying with me in the dorm, and she had the baby—earlier than expected. We didn't have a chance to get her to the hospital. Anyway, I want to take her to Yong's mother so she can take care of them."

"Where's Yong?" Ming demands. "He should take her."

"She's not with him anymore."

Ming rolls his eyes. "I'm not surprised. I tried to tell you that he was trouble. She was stupid to expect him to stay with her once she became an inconvenience."

My mouth twitches. Maybe he isn't jealous anymore, but his reaction tastes bitter.

"Why do you even want to help her? All that time she was gone, you kept looking for her, and she never got in touch with you." He leans in, anger and disgust in his eyes. "What kind of friend is that?"

I can feel the color rising to my face. I want to shout, *She isn't just a friend!* But I keep my mouth closed. We need him to help us.

"Why do you care so much about her?"

I stare at him in astonishment. The sharp yellow light of the floods light half his face, the other side shadowed by the windowless building. Maybe this is what's been keeping me from him—not that he wants Yun, but that he doesn't understand *me*. He has a family. And because he has one, he should understand. I'm trembling inside, wanting to explain but not trusting myself to find the right words.

I have to focus. Instead of responding to his question,

162

I say, "Yun says your cousin has a car."

He straightens up and tucks his chin back, caught off guard by the change in topic.

"Will you ask him to drive us?" I press. "Yellow Grain Village is only two or three hours away."

For several moments my question hangs in the air. "But it's Spring Festival. The worst time to travel!" Ming says.

"I know. I tried to get bus tickets, but there's nothing." I step closer to him. "I'll help pay for the gas. I've got plenty of money. If you could just—"

He cuts me off. "That's a big favor for me to ask my cousin. For you to ask of me! For Yun, of all people! You shouldn't have anything to do with her!"

I can feel him losing patience with Yun, with me.

But he's my best chance to get Yun out of the city. If she stays, she might give the baby away. I know I have to keep that baby. She and Yun are my family now. I steel myself.

"Yun says the baby is yours."

Ming steps back in open-mouthed silence, looking as if I've slapped him. For a moment I want to take it back, hating the lie, but I remind myself that it might be true. And Ming doesn't protest, doesn't say it's impossible.

Anyway, I know I have to push on. "She doesn't want you to have to carry that responsibility. She's not asking you to support the baby." I move forward to close the space between us. "Just help us get to Yong's ma. We'll tell Ma that the baby is Yong's, and she'll take care of it. She *wants* a baby! And Yong's in jail. No need to worry about him right now."

In the shadows, I can see him blinking, his eyes shifting side to side as he tries to make sense of everything I've said. His breath puffs from his mouth. I shiver, suddenly aware of the cold. Inwardly, I beg him not to ask me anymore questions, to just say he'll help us.

He nods, looking at the concrete between our feet as he mutters, "All right. I'll call my cousin tonight."

❖❖❖

The next morning I get a text from Ming: *My cousin can take you to Yellow Grain Village tomorrow. That's when his time off starts.*

I bite my lip and type a reply: *Thank you so much, Ming!* I hesitate a moment before adding, *Are you coming with us?*

It seems like ages before he responds. *No, but I'll cover for you with my dad so you don't get in trouble for missing your last day of work.*

I breathe out slowly, relief and nervousness tangled up inside me. I thank him again. He doesn't text back this time.

❖❖❖

Yun, Ming, and I cross the factory plaza during the morning shift change. We have to walk slowly for Yun's sake and try not to attract attention, but that's impossible. Even though people have their heads bent against the bits of ice that rain down, everyone notices the baby. Yun wanted to put the baby in an unzipped duffle bag to make her easier to carry, but I pulled a face at the idea and told her I would carry her to the car.

Now I see that Yun's idea had its merits. The baby is no problem to carry, isn't even crying, but everyone we pass gapes at us, their eyes darting from the baby, to me, to Yun beside me. The girls about our age are surprised and delighted, while the older workers glare knowingly at me, since I'm the one carrying her.

164

Ming carries our bag, but no one notices him because he walks several feet apart from us. I'm glad he doesn't have to deal with the rude stares. A lump rises in my throat as I think of how I lied to him.

We pass through the factory gates and go down the street toward the corner. I see Ming casting sidelong glances at the baby and Yun. He hasn't said anything more about the baby—hasn't even asked if it's a boy or a girl, though her pink dotted blanket probably answers that question for him.

Ming's cousin pulls up as we reach the corner. Yun climbs in first and gingerly scoots across. I hand the baby to her. As I start to get in, though, Ming puts his hand on my arm.

"Wait." He chucks my bag in the front seat, then turns his dark-eyed gaze on me. "Is there any chance for us?"

My breath catches at this unexpected question. Swiftly, I see us getting married, in our own room, with our own baby. I'm so happy that he wants me, that he's asking me to forget the past. But I also know I've deceived him, used him. My mouth opens—no words come out. I want to say yes, but the truth is that I don't know.

CHAPTER 26

Yun

The drive should only take a couple of hours, but the highways are clogged with lines of hardly-moving traffic. Ming's cousin opens the window an inch to let out his cigarette smoke, but because we're stopped, the smoke and exhaust fumes filter in and create smog inside the car. All around us people punch out spurts of noise from their horns or lean on them loud and hard. Sometimes Ming's cousin mutters curses with his cigarette hanging from his lip. He grips the wheel and veers onto the slushy shoulder, where the wintry air bites our cheeks. When he comes up behind another car riding the shoulder, he tries to nose back onto the road, blasting the horn. The baby cries, getting red in the face, and Ming's cousin tells us to hold her up to the windows until one of the other drivers takes pity on us and lets us back onto the road.

Luli fusses over the baby, whispering to her, awkwardly changing her diapers in the little space between us. The car is foul. Even with the cold, damp air blowing in through the window, I can still smell the dirty diapers balled up on the floorboards, the overflowing ashtray, and the musty vinyl.

The smells, the snow, the traffic. The baby screaming in the car. I feel numb to it. I doze several times, waking to see

Luli smiling down at the baby with her soft-eyed expression, or studying me anxiously. When she looks at me, I turn away to the window.

After several hours, as we get farther from the city, the traffic moves a little more easily. It's not so flat here now, and the air seems cleaner, though the sky is still overcast. At least the views are more interesting. I can see two- and three-story block houses, spaced widely apart, kids in puffed coats with sticks, jabbing at the dirty snow. I realize I've ridden on this road three times now—with Yong on his motorbike, on the bus back to the city, and here again. The car hums on the pavement, and I feel like I'm going somewhere, returning somewhere. I just want to sleep and watch TV and eat the food that Ma makes—all the things the girls in the factory say they do when they go home.

By now the baby has fallen asleep. "Could you hold her for a while?" Luli whispers to me. "My arms are getting tired." She wakes when Luli passes her over, but she doesn't cry. I set her on my legs, and she's warm against me, her dark little eyes watchful, roving around. I wonder what she sees. Her eyes fix on me, and her mouth makes a pink o shape. I wonder if she knows who I am.

"What should we name her?" Luli asks, fingering the baby's hand.

Naming her hasn't even occurred to me.

"How about Chun, Spring? Since it's the Spring Festival!" Luli grins. She strokes the baby's cheek. "Hello, little Chun. Fu Chun."

"Fu?" I wince. "Maybe not my last name."

"Why not?" Luli wrinkles her nose. "I don't like the idea of giving her Yong's name. I suppose Ma will want that. But Fu, *good fortune*, sounds better."

I bristle. "*Fu* isn't good luck. It's *Fu* from *fuliyuan*, orphanage—the opposite of good luck!" My voice is louder than I intended. The baby begins to twitch, and I can see Ming's cousin raise his eyebrows in the rearview mirror. "You have this name and everyone knows you're from an orphanage! Everyone knows nobody wanted you. They won't hire you because they think you're bad luck!"

Luli's lower lip draws in and she seems to shrink back in the seat. I can't believe that all this time she thought all the foundlings were named Fu for good luck. My ears are hot at the thought.

The baby starts crying, thrashes out her arms, kicks against her blanket. I flush, not knowing what to do. I'm afraid she's going to slip through my hands and slide off my knees. "Take her! Take her!"

Luli grabs the baby, hugs her to her chest, and sways side to side with her. She asks me to get the bottle, but I pretend I don't hear. I stare out the window, pulling on my hair. But I can hear Luli, humming and whispering to the baby until she begins to settle.

♦♦♦

We arrive in Yellow Grain Village by the late afternoon, when the cloud cover is starting to break up and the sun is actually visible. The trip has taken almost six hours. I don't know what I feel. Part of me is eager to see Ma, but part of me is a little scared. I don't know why I'm nervous. I know Luli was right when she said Ma would be happy that I'm bringing her a baby. Even if it's a girl. I know Ma will want to keep it.

Maybe I hate that she won't be able to. Not if Yong has anything to say about it.

I direct Ming's cousin to Ma's alley, and we pull up in front of her house. When I knock at the door, Ma opens it. She's wearing several layers of sweaters topped with a padded vest that does little to hide her thinness.

"You came back!" She throws her arms up in the air, her eyes full of relief.

"Ma, this is my friend Luli . . ." I trail off, not sure how to say the rest.

Her gaze flutters to each of us, finally landing on the baby in Luli's arms.

"Is this my baby?" She plucks her out of Luli's arms and begins rocking her. Her mouth is wide open, adoring the baby. "When did you have her? Oh, then she's early. Is everything all right with her?" She hurls out questions without letting me answer. "A girl then. Don't worry, you're young! You can try again since it's a girl." She spins into the room and her voice gentles. "Don't worry, we'll get you a brother," she says to the baby. She waves us to come inside. "Hurry up and shut the door. This little thing doesn't need to get sick."

Luli and I glance at each other. Luli has such a look of happiness on her face. As if everything has worked out just as she hoped.

Ming's cousin follows us inside, carrying the bag Luli packed for us. Faint slants of light stream in from the window, and I can see the dust motes floating in the small, cluttered room. My things are piled on the bed at the back of the room, and I let out a squeak of happiness. It's good to see my things, good to see Ma so happy.

"I'll drop this off and leave now." Ming's cousin puts the bag down just inside the door.

"Come in. Drink some tea." Ma glances up and waves him toward the table near the stove.

"Don't bother. Now that I see the girls are safely delivered, I should get going. Traffic's terrible, so I want to get started right away."

We thank him and he leaves. Ma holds the baby on her shoulder while she puts on the tea for us.

"Come on! Come on! Don't just stand there!" Ma barks at us until we start to take off our shoes. The room is cold enough to leave on our coats. We move to the stools at the table.

"What happened at the police station?" Ma demands. "That was very irresponsible! Running away like that! So much trouble for me, between Yong and you!" She shakes her head while she claps mugs onto the table in front of us.

"But you came back to me." She gives me a one-sided smile. I can tell she isn't mad. "And at just the right time!" She grins, showing all her brown teeth. "Wei's bringing Yong home soon!"

Luli draws in her breath sharply. Her happy smile is swept away, as if she's been dashed with cold dishwater.

"Wei thinks he has enough money for Yong's fine!" Ma takes no notice of our reaction as she juggles the baby and drops tea leaves in the cups. "Just in time for Spring Festival! Couldn't be more lucky, even though it's a terrible thing having to borrow money just before the holiday. But that's old-fashioned thinking, eh? Everyone will be home together!"

Luli's eyes are boring into me. I'm sure she wants to know what we're going to do when Yong shows up. I shrug to show her it doesn't matter, but my own mind races. I didn't think I would see Yong so soon. Not until I was sure what to do about the baby. Now, I'll have to decide before he gets back. Otherwise he might decide for me.

"If the police will just accept the money, they'll ride Yong's motorbike here. They could be back here tonight!" Ma says.

Luli begins to tremble.

"The roads are so busy. It took us six hours to get here," I say to Ma, but I'm speaking for Luli's benefit. "They probably won't make it tonight."

"A few hours won't matter so much," Ma says. "I hope Yong will forgive us for taking so long to get the money. Poor boy. He's had such a hard time."

The kettle is boiling, and she pours the water into the cups, still holding tightly to the baby with one arm. "If only I had been able to raise the money for the fines so I could get his hukou. But when my husband got sick, there was so much debt from his medicine and then his funeral." I've heard this story already, but Ma seems eager to repeat it for Luli's benefit. "Yong became a non-person. He couldn't go to school or get a decent position without his hukou. Always having to scramble for the worst kind of labor." She sniffs, tears coming to her eyes. "Wei and I always felt so terrible about it. It's not his fault he got mixed up with some bad people."

She sits at the table with the baby, hugging her to her chest and rocking her like Luli did in the car, as if soothing herself. "Don't worry, little one. You'll have your hukou."

My stomach twists. Ma still doesn't know, or won't let herself believe, that Yong and I aren't married. I can't bring myself to tell her that there are thousands of yuan in fines standing between this baby and a hukou.

Ma waves us to drink. Luli does as she's told, but I stand up and go to my things. I pull out some of my own clothes.

"You left without your bags! I kept everything for you. I knew you would be back." Ma is gleeful that she was right.

I can't wait to put on clean clothes. I've been wearing the same ones for so long. Luli wanted me to put some of hers on, but they wouldn't fit because my middle is still thick.

I pull the curtain across the bed to give myself some privacy, change my clothes, and chuck the dirty ones on the floor.

I come out from behind the curtain, but Ma flaps me back toward the bed.

"You have to drink some hot water. It's terrible you exposed yourself to the cold! But I am glad you came. Now you can have a proper sitting-in-the-month time. No more cold things, no bathing, no hair washing. Stay in bed. You have to rest at least the month to recover properly. I'll take care of you. I'll make you soup as soon as I can get some pigs' feet."

I climb into the bed, and she puts a steaming cup into my hands. I'm bone-tired, but I manage to give her a tiny smile. It's good to see Ma.

I decide I'm looking forward to seeing Yong too. Not because I want to be with him. That's all over now. But because I know he'll want to sell the baby. And I need him to let me in on the sale.

Through the gap in the curtains, I glance at Ma and Luli at the table. They're ogling the baby, so happy. I'll be sorry to take her away from them. I think of how Luli was when she first came to the orphanage—her sad, sad expression. The same look when she watched me leave the Institute. And Ma will surely have a fit of crying and screaming.

But I don't know how to be a mother. And even if Ma agrees to raise the baby, the fines we would have to pay for her to have a normal life would trap us for years, decades. None of us would have any sort of life outside of working, saving, worrying.

I know Ma and Luli want to help, but all of this is really my problem.

I'll tell them that the baby will have an easier life. Though I wonder if that's true, because Yong isn't trustworthy. He does whatever's best for himself, no matter what it means for other people. I know, because I'm like that too.

CHAPTER 27

Luli

All morning I'm nervous as a cat, dreading Yong's arrival. My ears are tuned to the alley, listening for his motorbike, and I jump at every sound. When I drop my mug at the table, Ma throws me an irritated look and tells me to get Yun's dirty clothes ready to wash. I'm grateful for something to distract me.

I go over to the bed, where Yun sits sipping the tea Ma brought her, and pick her clothes up from the floor.

"There are more dirty ones in that blue bag," Yun says.

"Check through all the pockets," Ma adds. "Then get that basin by the door and soak the clothes. When I get back from the market, I'll teach you how to do the wash. You girls who've grown up in the city! Now you'll have to learn to work!"

I glance back at Yun, and she makes a face. I smother a laugh.

"Ma, we know how to do laundry and all that sort of work from the Institute," Yun says. "And the factory."

Ma hoots. "I guess that's true. You probably even know how to take care of babies, maybe better than me. So take care of this one while I run to the market." She picks up Chun and nuzzles her before setting her back into the basket she found for her to sleep in. "I'll be back as soon as I can. No more than thirty minutes."

She leaves, and I start digging through the pockets of Yun's clothes. From a pair of jeans, I pull out a crinkled piece of paper. It's a business card. *Xiang Jian, Private Detection Services.*

"What's this?" I ask Yun, holding up the card.

Yun takes it from me and examines it. "Oh. The private detective. He came looking for Yong months ago. About some girl."

I suck in my breath. Every fear I have about Yong, about what he does for a living, about what kind of person he is, spikes to a new level. "Did he find her? Is that how Yong got caught and sent to jail?"

"I don't know." Yun crumples the card and tosses it beside her on the blankets. A moment later she gets up, puts her mug on the table, and snaps on the TV.

I snatch up the card and smooth it out. I look at Yun, wanting to know more, but she sinks into a chair in front of the TV and turns the volume up. Chun begins to fuss at the noise. I fold the card into my pocket and go to the baby.

◆◆◆

Late in the afternoon, I'm taking down the dry laundry from the line strung across the room when I hear a motorbike outside. My throat tightens. I listen as it comes closer in the alley and sputters to a stop. Clutching the shirt I've been folding against my chest, I turn to watch the door.

It flies open and Yong bursts in. "Ma! I'm—" He sees us, and his words fall off. His hair is matted and greasy, his upper lip and jawline marked with stubble. His eyes fly from me, to Yun stretched out on the bed with a magazine, to Ma at the stove with Chun.

"Yong! My boy! My boy! You're home now!" Ma flaps her arm at him. Another guy—Wei, I suppose—comes up behind him in the doorway, carrying a bag. His head is wrapped in a scarf. He sees us over Yong's shoulder and hesitates before he nudges Yong to move in. He shuts the door behind them, cutting off the flow of cold air.

"Look here! Look who's here!" Ma holds up Chun and skirts around the table and stools to get to Yong.

Yong looks from Chun to Yun, who sits up and swings her legs onto the floor. "Is it . . . ?"

"Yes! Yes! You're a father now!" Ma thrusts the baby up toward his face. She twists around and gestures to Yun with her elbow. "She did a good job. This little one is perfect."

"Girl or boy?" Yong asks Yun over Ma's head.

Yun gives no hint of how she feels. Her mouth twitches slightly, but before she says anything, Ma answers. "Girl. But don't worry. That just means you can try again. You'll have to wait a few years, but you'll be older then. And this one will help us take care of the other."

I'm holding my breath, not sure what kind of reaction to expect.

Yong's expression is as blank as Yun's. Stepping around Ma and Chun, he drops into the vinyl armchair in front of the television, his back to us. He rifles through the scattered mess of newspapers and magazines on the TV stand, probably searching for the remote. Without turning around, he says, "There are a lot of people who want to adopt a baby girl if it's healthy. I know I can find her a nice family that will pay. So many people

176

don't want to have to go through all the hassle of the Children's Social Welfare Institute."

A small cry escapes me. This is exactly what I was afraid he'd say. I look desperately at Yun, Wei, and Ma. Yun doesn't say anything. Wei, who has taken off his scarf and gloves, stands near the door rubbing his hands together, looking miserable and cold.

But Ma flies across the room to plant herself in front of Yong. "Shut your mouth! Why are you talking like that?" She glowers at him. "You aren't taking this baby anywhere! I'm keeping her right here, and when she gets older she'll take care of me, and probably you too!"

"Ma! Forget about it!" Yong sits upright, raising his voice. "I don't want a child yet! And she"—he ticks his head toward Yun without turning around—"can't afford to keep it. The fines she'll have to pay!"

Ma frowns. "What are you talking about? What fines? What do you mean, she'll have to pay?"

"Ma." He tosses his head back dismissively. "Yun and I aren't married. I'm not responsible for that baby. And she'll be fined for having a baby without a permit."

Ma gasps and moves one hand around Chun as if to shelter the baby from such awful words.

"The fines will be at least five times her annual salary. Maybe more!" Yong twists around and throws an arm on the back of his chair, turning toward Yun. "I'm surprised they even allowed her to give birth!"

Ma's face seems to crumble like a building being demolished. "The child won't be able to get her hukou until the fines are paid!"

The baby begins to squall. I rush over and try to take her from Ma, but she clutches her harder.

"All the trouble of this life when a child has no hukou!" Ma moans. "That's what got *you* into all your trouble!"

Yong ignores her. He finds the remote and snaps on the television. The blare of it fills the room.

My heart is twisting. I want to get Yun alone so I can talk to her about what Yong said. I have to make sure she doesn't listen to him. I try to catch her eye, but she steadily watches Ma. I feel like she's avoiding me.

Ma steps in front of the TV, blocking Yong's view. "This is your child! You have to help her. Now look, with you and Wei—and Yun too in a few months—with everybody working, we can save all the money to cover the fines in just a few years!"

"We also have to pay back all the money we borrowed to get Yong out of jail," mumbles Wei.

"Yes, yes," says Ma impatiently, "but with the three of you working, by the time this one is ready for school, the fines will be paid."

Hope swells in my chest. If Ma believes we can make this work, there's still a chance.

"Four of us!" I say. I go to the bed and kneel next to Yun. "I can help too. And Ma can take care of the baby here, so the rest of us can work full time." I nod vigorously at Yun, urging her to agree.

She looks at me, at Yong, her face smooth as concrete, still not saying a word.

CHAPTER 28

Yun

Four of us, Luli says. Yong and Wei and I have no choice in it. I know Luli and Ma think they're solving our problems, but all they've done is commit us all to years of debt. I picture myself holed up in a factory dorm room, sending home all my money like Dali, eating tasteless canteen food every day, my life as gray and empty as it was at the Institute. I picture five, ten years of that. And I want to scream.

◆◆◆

For the next couple of days, Luli doesn't leave Yong and me alone for a moment—which isn't difficult in Ma's small house. Since she's volunteered to help with the baby, Ma's happy to let her stay here through the holiday. The three of us cram together in Ma's bed at night, and during the day Luli pitches in with the housework and the baby's care.

She never talks when Yong is around, but she's watchful of him. Her eyes constantly flick to him watching television, cracking melon seeds between his teeth, texting on his mobile. Her expression is dead solemn. Only when he goes out to make a phone call or to visit his old friends does she become cheerful, chattering to the baby. I know she doesn't want Yong and me left alone. And she never leaves the baby except when she goes to the toilet.

Wei is in and out of the house, usually wearing an expression that makes it clear how much he regrets coming home in the first place. On our third morning here, Wei goes out to buy firecrackers. Ten minutes later Ma exclaims, "Oi! I'm almost out and I need to start making our Spring Festival dumplings! I forgot to tell Wei."

I don't react to this. I know Ma won't expect *me* to do anything. I'm wrapped in the comforter from the bed, sitting sideways in the vinyl chair near the TV, rotating through shows with the remote. Aside from the TV, the room is dim, with only a feeble light from the window beside the door.

Yong, sitting at the table eating a late breakfast amid everyone else's empty plates, keeps shoveling food in his mouth. Ma never asks him to help her out either.

"Luli," Ma says as she drops another scoop of food onto Yong's plate, "run and get it for me, before the stores get too crowded."

Luli is holding the baby, bouncing her lightly. She hesitates. Glances at Yong, who pushes away his plate and lights a cigarette.

"Okay," Luli agrees after a moment. She sets the baby down just long enough to shrug on her coat. Then she takes the baby over to the bed, gets her bag, and pulls out the baby's own tiny purple coat. The baby kicks and makes her burble noises as Luli puts the coat on her, expertly directing her arms through the sleeves before pinching together the snaps. I know those moves myself. We dressed so many babies at the orphanage. But Luli smiles so sweetly at the baby, her eyes shine with such tenderness, that I only feel the hole in my heart more strongly.

"What are you doing?" Ma says to Luli as she waves away smoke coming from Yong's cigarette.

"Just getting her ready."

Ma leaves the mess at the table and goes to pick up the baby. Luli is quick to reach over and take her out of Ma's hands.

"I'm taking Chun with me." Luli pivots and swiftly crosses the room.

"No! You're not thinking!" Ma sounds shocked. "It's cold enough to snow today. The wind is too harsh. No baby should be outside. Especially one who's only a few days old!"

Luli glances out the window but doesn't say anything. She slips her feet into her shoes and bends awkwardly to put a finger in the heel while still holding the baby.

Ma shuffles over in her slippers, flapping her hands at the baby. "Give her to me. You can't take her out there."

Luli turns her back to Ma and throws the door open. Cold air scours in as she rushes out. Her coat is gapped open. She didn't even have time to snap the buttons.

"Stop!" Ma cries. "The baby! The baby! It's too cold!" She steps out into the street, but a moment later she runs back in and grabs her coat. "Stupid girl! She doesn't know anything. The cold! The germs!" In a fluster, she works on her coat and rushes back out, still in her slippers. She fights against the wind to get the door closed behind her. Even with it shut, I can hear her shouting after Luli as she chases her down the lane.

Ma and Luli truly love that baby. I feel a pang in my chest. I try to sigh it away.

Yong, still at the table, snickers. His cigarette is a stub, and he grinds it out in a dirty dish, then comes over and perches on the metal armrest of my chair.

He gives me his lazy smile. "Alone, finally!" He puts his arm around me and leans down.

I let him kiss me, even opening my mouth a little and tasting his ashiness, but after a moment I pull back. The light from the television flashes off his face. He looked as bad as a vagrant when he first arrived, but having shaved and washed, he looks like his old self, despite the morning stubble and his hair poking in all directions from sleep. He's still good-looking. But I feel nothing for him. "Forget it," I say. "We're all done with that."

He gives me a disgusted scowl, like he doesn't believe it.

Before he can get angry or even say anything, I ask, "What about the baby, then?"

I'm not stupid enough to think he's going to pitch in to pay my fines. Ma might have convinced herself that we'll be one big family working together to give this baby a good life, but I know better.

He glares at me for a moment longer before he shifts off my chair and flops into the other one. "I think my boss has found someone to take her."

Anger flares through me, even though this is exactly what I expected. He's gone ahead and started making arrangements before we've even talked about it. I set my mouth hard. "How much will they give us?"

He raises his eyebrows. I know it's the *us* he's questioning.

"I want half of the money," I say. "I need it until I get a new position."

"I'll have to split it with the boss," he says, "and I have to give Wei and Ma the money to pay back what they borrowed."

I tug at my hair. I doubt he'll do it. He's more likely to take the money and go back to the city, leaving me stranded here.

It flashes through my mind: Ma kicking me out of the house once the baby's gone, me with no job and nowhere to live.

I have to make sure I get my share. Without it, I have no hope of getting back on my feet.

"If you don't give me my half of the money, I'll tell Ma what you're going to do."

He snorts out a laugh and shrugs. I know that was a stupid thing to say. Ma can scream and cry, but she can't stop him. Yong is her boy, and she'll forgive him whatever he does.

"The police then!" I thrust my chin out. "You want to go back to jail? I'll report you to the Public Security Bureau for kidnapping and *human trafficking*!"

His mouth turns small. He gives me a murderous look. I stare right back at him. I'm not going to give in.

"You said it could be a lot of money. There'll be enough for both of us. After it's done, we don't have to have anything else to do with each other."

He draws out another cigarette from the pack in his shirt pocket. "If it's money you want—real money, I mean—brides bring five times as much as babies." Rather than lighting the cigarette, he toys with it, first holding it at the ends with the tips of his fingers, then wobbling it between his thumb and forefinger.

My skin prickles and turns hot. He's talking about selling me. I shouldn't be surprised—I shouldn't even be outraged—but I can't help it. Maybe some part of me has refused to believe that Yong would see me like this. As a business opportunity, as something he can turn into money. But of course, if I'm smart, I'll start thinking the same way.

I force myself to think about this calmly. "Are you offering me a deal?" I ask. "You'd split the profits?"

He shrugs. "Sure."

I play this out in my head—not for the first time, but more seriously than I ever have before. He'd deliver me to some farmer, and then I could run away. But he would be leaving me behind, taking the money with him. There's no way I could trust him to give me my share once I got away. I scoff out loud and shake my head.

"What?" he says. "I'm not kidding. Eight thousand yuan is nothing to laugh about. And a home for a girl with no family, someone too shy to find her own husband." His brows go up, and he rolls his eyes and head toward the door in a pointed gesture.

For a long minute, I'm aware only of the pulsing roar in my ears as his meaning sinks in. *No family. Shy.* He's not planning to sell me after all. He's talking about Luli.

Luli *is* shy, timid really. And much too trusting. She wouldn't know how to fight or lie or escape from her buyer.

Yong must've been sizing her up ever since he came home. All this time she's been watching him, worried about the baby, worried about me, while he's been thinking about kidnapping her.

I'm tempted to let loose a string of curses and fly at Yong, but for once I hold back. My mind scrambles to figure out how to get him to leave her out of this, how to turn this mess around.

"I can be shy," I say. I'm aware my voice sounds gruff and pushy.

"Ha!" He laughs and lights his cigarette.

"I can! For that kind of money, I can." I muster up a demure smile. It feels unconvincing. Yong makes a face at my bad acting, but he's amused. Quickly, I go back to talking about the baby to make him forget about Luli. "If you have it arranged for the baby, let's go ahead with it. You'll give me half, and you can tell your boss that I'll marry one of his country bumpkins.

When he gets that set up, we'll figure out how you'll get my share of the money to me."

He studies me for a long time, his mouth pursed. I look right back at him, my heart thumping in my chest. He finally takes a long drag on his cigarette, and shifts his eyes to the television.

I figure that means he's agreed. I know I'll still have to make sure he gives me my half of the baby money before I disappear. I have no intention of going along with his bride scheme. As soon as the baby's taken care of and I have what he owes me, Luli and I are getting out of here.

The door opens. Ma, holding the baby, charges in with another gust of icy wind. "Who takes a baby out in cold like this! The wind is driving the dust like a sandstorm. And some boys down the next lane are ready to set off fireworks too!"

Luli comes in a few seconds later. Her eyes dart to Ma, to Yong, to me. I quickly turn away so she won't see the guilt pinching in my chest. I remind myself that Yong would've taken the baby anyway; none of us could've stopped him. I'm only trying to make the best of this hopeless situation.

"What are you doing back already?" Ma asks Luli. She takes the baby with her to a stool and plops down. "Where's the oil?"

Luli doesn't answer. She's rooted in place, blinking at us like a turtle. I can feel her gaze going back and forth between Yong and me even as I stare at the TV, watching two young women teeter on high heels as they try to stomp balloons on a game show.

"So stupid to come back without the oil!" Ma snaps. "I won't be able to cook without it. Go on!" Luli's shoulders stiffen and she goes back out the door.

My whole body aches with exhaustion. I wish none of this had happened, but it has, and now I just want it to be done.

CHAPTER 29

Luli

I march to the public toilets at the end of the lane. The wind is harsh and gritty, so I go around to the west side of the structure and hunker against it. Despite the faint scent of coal smoke coming from the stovepipes on the roofs and the snuffling of some pigs penned nearby, I'm struck by the cleanness of the air and the quiet of the lane. The memory of Granddad rushes back, and for a moment I feel like I'm back in my old home. I blink back tears, thinking how different my life was then, before Granddad got sick.

I pull out my phone and nervously punch out the number I memorized days ago.

The voice that answers is deep-toned and curt. "Xiang Investigations."

Never having spoken to a private investigator, I'm not sure what to say. I hesitate.

"Hello?"

"Yes. My name is Cao Luli. I'm . . . I'm calling about someone you were looking for. Liang Yong."

"What is it?"

"He's here. Yong's here in Yellow Grain Village with his ma and . . . us."

"Liang Yong was caught with his associate and turned over to police last week."

"Yes, yes, but he's out now! He bribed his way out and came home to his ma. We had come too, just before he arrived, Yun and I with the baby, not knowing he was coming. You spoke with her—Yun—once. You tried to warn her but she didn't listen! She had a baby, his baby. And now he wants to sell her!"

The line is quiet on the other end, although I feel as if I can hear Mr. Xiang sizing up the situation. He's silent for so long that I start to wonder if I've made a mistake. Maybe he's not going to help me. A panicky feeling overtakes me, as bad as the day Granddad's neighbor left me at the orphanage. I feel hot tears filming my eyes. Words gush out of me.

"I'm calling for Yun. She begged me to. She just had the baby and it was bloody and difficult. She's too sick to call you herself. Not just sick, but crazy with worry that Yong is going to take the baby and sell her any day now!"

The lies and half-truths tumble from my mouth. It's as if *I'm* the Yun I'm speaking of. I'm blubbering now, snot dripping from my noise, my tears freezing on my face in the cold. I know I'm hardly making sense, but I grasp for anything to say, anything that will make him help me. I tell him Yun named the baby Chun. That Yong didn't want to get married. And that Yong started looking for a buyer right away, has probably already located one. "He'll tear Chun away from her mother who loves her. For money! It would kill Yun!"

I sob. Deep-gutted sobs that shake my body. "I have money. We have money to pay you. Please, can't you do something?"

Detective Xiang's voice crackles over the line. He says he'll drive to Yellow Grain Village. He'll have to wait until something actually happens before he can intervene, but at least he is coming.

CHAPTER 30

Yun

Four days later, Spring Festival has come and gone. Wei pieces together some rides and heads back to work in Gujiao to make up for the time he lost getting Yong out of jail.

A couple hours after Wei leaves, I notice Yong furtively gathering up his stuff—his phone charger, a jacket he always leaves draped over a kitchen chair. While Ma's busy cooking and Luli is out using the toilet, I whisper, "So you found a buyer?"

Irritation flashes across his face. "Keep your voice down."

"I am. When are you going to take her?"

"Tonight."

I nod. "Okay. I'll take my share of the money now."

His frown deepens. "I don't have it yet. I won't get paid till I've made the delivery."

"Fine. Then I'll go with you tonight."

"What? No."

"Either you front me the cash now, or I go along and get paid when you do."

He narrows his eyes at me, trying to scare me into backing down, but I only say, "Unless you want me to report you?"

That settles it.

In the dead of that night, I hear the creak of Yong's bedroom door. The nightlight by the bed throws shadows as Yong comes through and puts a finger to his lips.

I slip noiselessly out of bed and pause to make sure I haven't disturbed Ma and Luli. Luli's smooth face has a faint line at her forehead, as if she's having a bad dream. Ma snores softly. A twinge catches in my throat, but I swallow it down.

Yong clicks on a flashlight and sweeps it low across the room. He picks up the baby in her basket while I put on my coat and shoes and grab my purse. We're at the door when we hear a distant crack of fireworks. The baby shifts in her basket. I glance back at the bed, but Ma and Luli don't move. Spring Festival is over, but people are still setting off their leftover bangers. I'm used to the noise.

We steal outside. I wind my arms around myself and shiver in the wind that whips along the alley. Overhead, only a tiny slash of moon is visible in the black sky. I hold the flashlight for Yong as he straps the baby's basket to the motorbike in front of the seat. After he straddles the bike and jounces it off its kickstand, I edge sideways onto the seat behind him, wincing with soreness. He starts up the engine. The baby starts to whimper.

The door to Ma's house swings wide, and Luli is there in her T-shirt and long underwear. Her clothes are too thin, rippling in the cold wind, but she stands there, with her bare arms at her sides, as if she doesn't feel the cold. I have the strange thought that even though I'm yards away, I can feel heat coming off her body.

Someone sets off more firecrackers on another lane, the pops echoing off the brick of the buildings. Yong guns the throttle and we take off, but I peer back at Luli, her face pale and white. The light comes on in the house, framing her and Ma, who crowds into the doorway with a blanket over her shoulders. Right away, she's yanking on Luli's arm, nearly pulling her over.

I want to shout to them that it's better this way. That the baby will have a better home. That we won't have to worry about money. That now we can go back to how things were before.

But we round the corner, and they're out of sight before any words came out.

CHAPTER 31

Luli

Once they've turned out of the lane and I know which way they've gone, I bolt back into the house. Ma trails me, screaming, "What's happened? Where are they going? Where are they taking the baby?"

I don't answer. Instead, I fling the blankets off the bed, searching for my mobile.

"Luli, tell me what's happening!"

I find my phone and punch out Mr. Xiang's number. I turn away from Ma, covering my ear to block out her voice.

He answers on the second ring.

"He's taken the baby!" I shout into the phone so he can hear me over Ma's wailing.

"How long ago? Which way?"

"Just now. He turned left, away from the village center!"

Mr. Xiang clicks off, but I keep listening to the dial tone for several moments. Ma collapses onto the bed, moaning, begging me to tell her what's going on.

I barely hear her. When I was outside watching Yun and Yong drive off, I didn't notice the frigid wind, but now, as I stand in the middle of Ma's house, my blood suddenly feels like ice.

I know that Yun's time in the Institute has damaged some part of her, for babies, for feeling. I feared she would give up Chun, but I never imagined that she would go with Yong herself. I hoped to save Chun by calling Mr. Xiang, but what will happen to Yun when Mr. Xiang catches up with them?

CHAPTER 32

Yun

We speed along the hills with only the single headlight to show the way. Every bounce on the rutted dirt roads hurts me between my legs, my back in its twisted position, my tailbone. I can feel the blood draining from me. I know it's stupid to go with Yong, but I know he won't give me the money otherwise.

The wind stings my face. I feel as if I'll die with cold. Ma would scold terribly that I'm making myself sick and ruining my health forever. Well, she probably won't care about me anymore. She'll think only of the baby. I glance over Yong's shoulder, trying to see the baby in her basket, but the white slice of moon doesn't give enough light. Ma would be so wrecked to hear how she cries out in the cold, her short, ragged bleats. She would say I'm going to get her killed this way. My chest aches. People have often let me know I'm a worthless person, but now I feel I'm a terrible one.

I keep seeing Ma and Luli in my head, the way they looked as we drove away. I've never seen Luli with that expression on her face, so still, so hard. I have no idea what she was thinking. I wonder if she hates me now. If she'll forgive me when I go back. And Ma. She'll be so mad. Without the baby, there's nothing to hold her to me. I didn't think that would bother me so much.

It doesn't matter anyway, because I'll be going back to the city, and I'll throw myself back into working.

We hit smoother roads, and the baby slowly quiets until she finally falls asleep. I would go to sleep myself, but I'm afraid of falling off the bike.

When the sky begins to lighten, I hear the baby start to bawl again. At first, Yong just drives faster as if to drown her out with the sound of the engine, but she doesn't let up. I glimpse her red, squalling face poking out of the thick swaddling. One of her hands has fought past all the layers, and her tiny fingers move as if she's trying to claw her way out. She must be hungry. My breasts hurt, though I thought my milk had dried up.

I tap Yong on the shoulder. "We have to stop somewhere and get her some formula." I didn't think to bring any.

Yong half turns his head and shouts back to me, "Nothing will be open this early."

The baby continues screaming, grating my nerves. Luli or Ma would have picked her up, rocked her, rubbed her back, chanted her name—*Chun, Chun, Chun*. I would do it myself if we were stopped. I sigh. I'm tired and aching so deeply, inside and out, all over.

The sun creeps up over the hills. At last her cries weaken to the faintest whimper. "You'd better find a store!" I shout to Yong. "Or the baby will get sick and nobody will want her!"

He turns onto the potholed, winding streets of a little town. Soon we find a stall shop with its metal door rolled up, revealing towering piles of household goods. Yong stops the bike. I glance at Chun. Her eyes are slightly open, but she isn't making any noise. Her face and lips look bloodless. I flinch. The rows of sick babies at the Institute flit into my mind. I'm glad I made Yong stop.

He hands me four yuan. I stiffly slide off the bike and hobble over to the stall as quickly as I can. All sorts of products are stacked against the walls and piled on the long table in the center—black plastic men's slippers, towels, colored basins, brooms. I edge toward the back, scanning for foodstuffs or baby things.

And that's when I hear the motorbike start up and speed away.

CHAPTER 33

Luli

"Luli, tell me! Tell me! Where are they going? Who were you talking to?" Ma demands.

I don't want to talk to her. I just want to think.

But Ma won't let up. She pleads and yanks on my clothes until I finally burst out, "They've taken the baby to sell."

"Not true! Not true!" Ma screams and slaps at my arms. "You're lying!"

I move away from her, shaking my head. "Why would I lie? Yun is my closest friend. She's all I have in the world. Do you think I want to believe she would do this?"

Ma stares at me. For a moment I'm afraid she's going to come at me again, but she just drops into a chair and wails.

I feel sorry for her now. Her son has done something unforgivable. And I know just how she feels, because my friend has done the same thing.

I go to her and crouch next to the chair. "Ma, there's a chance we'll get her back. I called a private detective. That's who I was talking to. He's gone after them. He'll find them."

Her face is a mess. "A detective! What about Yong? What will happen to him?"

I bite my lips. "Maybe . . ." I think about saying that maybe the detective will just collect the baby and let Yun and Yong go free. But I don't want Yong to go free. And I doubt he will after what he's done. I can't give Ma false hope. "Ma, the important thing is that he'll bring Chun back to us. Let's just think about the baby."

I keep repeating this, trying to calm her, convince her. Convince myself. Finally I say, "It's late. You should try to get some sleep. We'll know more in the morning." I help her into bed. As I pile on the covers, she looks at my arms, still slightly red where she hit me. Her face crumbles again and she grasps my hands, then starts rubbing my arms. Her hands are warm against my cold, goose-fleshed skin.

"Luli, forgive me. I shouldn't have done that. I wasn't thinking." Her tears have slowed but are still leaking down her face. "You're trying to help. I know that. You're a good girl."

Nobody's called me that in a long, long time. I hold in a sob.

Ma eventually falls asleep, but I can't. I stay at the table clutching my phone, hoping and not hoping for a call from Mr. Xiang, worrying about what I may have done to Yun. Will he arrest her? Maybe he won't find them. But then Chun would be lost to us. Maybe she'll go to a good home . . .

I'm twisted in knots wondering if I did the right thing. Every scenario crosses my mind. Maybe Yong tricked Yun into going with him. Does he plan on selling her as well? In my heart, I know that Yun chose to go, to get the money. I truly don't believe she means to stay with Yong, but I am sure she's in danger.

I see now that Yun will always be reckless, and maybe it's better that the baby goes to someone else. But it's too late to undo the call to Mr. Xiang. Too late to do anything but wait and see what happens next.

My knuckle is raw from where I've been digging my teeth into it. I'm longing to talk to someone. Impulsively, I scroll for Ming's number and push the call button. The phone rings four times before he answers. "Hello?" His voice is gravelly from sleep, and I remember that it's the middle of the night.

"Ming. It's Luli," I whisper. "I'm sorry, it's so late. I didn't think. Go back to sleep."

"What's the matter?"

"Nothing, nothing." Regret rushes over me. I lied to him about Chun being his so that he would help us get here. Before, I thought I was being strong in a desperate situation, but now I see that I was weak to use him. He's done so much, and I owe it to him to tell him the truth, but I know that now isn't the time. I hope I can make things right with him. When all this is over, I'll try, but right now there's too much to explain.

I push down my upset and try to sound normal. "I just wanted to hear your voice, but I didn't think about the time. Go back to sleep. Call me tomorrow."

I click off, feeling hollow inside. I'm wrung out with trying to fix this awful situation. Even stronger than the guilt about lying to Ming is the worry over what I've done to Yun. As messed up as she is, she's like family to me, and now, I may be sending her to prison. I never intended that. She doesn't deserve that. But I can't see any way to stop it.

CHAPTER 34

Yun

I stumble frantically out of the stall shop. By the time I reach the lane, Yong has already rounded a bend, leaving behind only a spray of dust and the distant rumble of the engine. I open my mouth to shout after him, but only a huff comes out. I feel as if I've been punched.

I look at the four yuan I clutch in my hand. All the money I have left.

"What are you looking for?" shouts a woman squatting at the back of the shop, pulling cans out of a cardboard box.

Formula. I think of the baby's pale lips. I curse Yong under my breath. If the baby dies . . . My head begins to pound. To drive out the thought, I grab fistfuls of my hair close to the scalp at my temples and tug. Babies can be tough little things, I tell myself. It will take more than just one day. This I know from the Institute.

"What's the matter?" The woman eyes me as she dusts the cans with a cloth and sets them on an already crowded shelf.

I don't know how to answer. *I'm hurt. I ran away. I tried to sell my baby. I was tricked. My baby has been kidnapped. I want to go home. I have no home.*

I only ask, "Is there a bus station?"

"Not in this village, but in the next town over." She waves her cloth to her left. "About four miles. Where are you going?"

I hesitate. I see myself showing up at Ma's, alone, without the baby. Luli will give me that cold, bitter stare so unlike her, and Ma will scream and scream at me. But it's the only place to go. And maybe I can at least get Luli away from there before Yong comes back and tries to take her too.

CHAPTER 35

Luli

When I hear a faint knock, I drop the knife on top of the cabbage I'm chopping for dinner and shoot across the room. I fling the door open, expecting Mr. Xiang, but instead it's Ming, giving me a hesitant half-smile.

The disappointment stings like a cut, and when Ming's smile vanishes, I'm aware that it shows on my face. But I am pleased to see Ming. I quickly rearrange my expression. "What are you doing here? It's so good to see you!" I gush as I pull him inside and shut the door.

He takes off his gloves, tucks them under his arm, and rubs his hands together to warm them. "My cousin brought me." He looks over my head, sees Ma, and gives her a polite nod. "You sounded so strange last night."

I feel a rush of tears springing up, the strain from the last few days about to spill out like an over-boiling pot.

Ma pushes up next to me. "Who's this?"

I put my hands up to my face, unable to speak.

"I'm Ming." He pastes a smile on his face. "Luli's friend from Gujiao. We work together." His voice falters, and I figure he's anxious because as far as he knows, he's Chun's father.

Ma's face falls. She goes back to the table and mechanically starts chopping again. Her lined face seems even more sagging and old than usual.

Ming lowers his voice. "Come outside. My cousin said he'll find a place to wait in the village center. You can walk over with me."

I hesitate, not wanting to leave in case Mr. Xiang shows up. But I nod and put my coat on. "I'm just going out for a minute," I tell Ma. She doesn't even look up.

Outside, the air is sharp and as raw as a slap, but the wind has died down. After the dimness of Ma's house, my eyes take a minute to adjust to the white brightness of the sky. When they do, I sweep my gaze to both ends of the lane, hoping for any sign of Mr. Xiang. All the brick houses are closed up tight against the cold, red couplets are pasted on the doors and windows, and tattered firecracker refuse litters the ground. "I can't go all the way to the village center with you," I say to Ming. "Can we talk here?"

"I understand," Ming answers, though he really doesn't. He steps closer to me. The bulk of him in his coat takes some of the keenness out of the cold. "You sounded so awful on the phone last night. When you called me, I thought . . . I guess I hoped you forgave me."

My heart squeezes. I want to explain the lie I told him, but my mind stumbles over where to start—how much to tell him about Yong, Yun, the baby sold, Mr. Xiang. He hasn't even asked about Chun.

"I'm sorry for the way I talked to you about Yun," Ming says. "At first I was mad when she got together with Yong, and I took that out on you. But now I don't care. It's you I care about." He gazes at me softly. "You were so isolated in that orphanage, I'm afraid that you're going to . . . get taken advantage of. Look at what happened to Yun." He averts his eyes and sighs. He must be thinking that her situation—fired, with a baby—is his fault. "Not that you're anything like Yun. It's just that it's . . . harder . . . more coldhearted outside."

"But Ming, there was nothing *but* coldheartedness at the Institute. That's why Yun is the way she is. I *am* different because I didn't start out there like she did. That's why I couldn't give up on her." Couldn't, meaning I have now.

His head drops and he studies the ground. He rubs what's left of a popper with his shoe. "Well, I'm sorry about Yun and me," he mutters. "I wish it had never happened."

He helped her get a position, helped both of us find jobs. I would probably be working in the Institute if he hadn't helped us. I can't wish it never happened. My stomach hurts. I have to tell him that I tricked him.

"You look so miserable." He reaches a hand up to my face and strokes my cheek.

I feel like crying. "I'm the one who should be sorry." I take a deep breath. "You may not be Chun's father. Yun doesn't know whether she's yours or Yong's. I told you that you were the father so you would help us. I'm so sorry I lied to you."

He lets his hand fall to his side. "Shit!" I watch as the look on his face goes from confusion, to astonishment, to . . . relief?

He cracks an openmouthed grin. White puffs of breath come out of his mouth in the cold. "Ha! I'll bet it isn't mine. I'm sure Yun is lying about not knowing whose it is." He flings his hand up in the air. "Luli, it's fine! I don't care! I don't care about the baby. I came here for you." He moves forward to close the gap between us, but I step back.

"What do you mean you don't care about the baby? What if it is yours?"

"It's not! You know Yun. But it doesn't matter. If Yong's ma wants it, she can keep it."

It hits me again that not once has he asked about Chun. I've been so torn up about lying to him that I didn't let it sink in. But now I'm beginning to see that he never had any feeling for Chun, even when he thought she was his. Chun isn't related to me at all, yet I'd still do anything to protect her. Ming hasn't been damaged the way Yun has. He's got no excuse for being this—this—*coldhearted*.

"Come back to Gujiao with me," Ming says. "My cousin is waiting with the car. You've done so much for Yun already, more than she deserves. Now you can put all this behind you and we can be together." He reaches his hands out to me.

I put my own hands behind my back.

He cocks his head at me. "Luli?"

A week ago I wanted so badly to be with him, to hear him tell me that he cared for me. But now all I can think is that I'm needed here, and he will never understand why.

I back away, slowly shaking my head. "You can go home now. Don't worry about me anymore. I'll be fine."

Confusion sweeps back across his face, along with something harder. "What? I came all the way out here and you're sending me away, just like that? After everything I've done for you?"

I bite my lip. "That's exactly why I'm asking you to leave. I'm grateful for all your help, but I can't take any more favors from you. I have to handle things on my own now."

My feelings are churning in a way I can't describe, but I turn and walk back inside, knowing I won't be sorry.

CHAPTER 36

Yun

I hurt so much that it takes more than two hours to walk to the next town. The blood flow that had started to slow the last couple days has turned heavy again, but I have several pads in my purse. I'm hungry, but I don't dare spend what little money I have. I want to make sure I have enough to buy the bus ticket.

When I finally get to the station, I find I can only afford to get to a town called Dusty Mountain. I'll have to walk the rest of the way to Ma's. But I'm lucky, because there's enough change from the ticket to buy a few buns, and I don't have to wait long for the bus. I sleep the whole way to Dusty Mountain.

At the next station, the ticket agent shows me the map and points to the towns and villages I'll pass on the way to Yellow Grain Village. He thinks it's eleven or twelve miles to get there and warns me that the roads are hilly.

I start walking in the midafternoon. The sun shines more brightly here in the countryside, and by this time of day, it's lowering in the hills and streaming directly into my eyes. I trudge along the road, glad of the numbing cold. Few people are out. Near the villages, ruddy-cheeked children gawk at me. Occasionally, I stop and ask for water. Someone runs inside and returns to hand me a cup.

I remember Ma saying there were no more young women in the countryside. All gone to work in the cities. I guess the ones I see now have returned for the holiday.

Ma really has been good to me. And Luli too. What did she say to me? *We've grown up together. We're like sisters.* I think about calling them, but I'm too scared. How would I explain myself? What would I say? The baby will be better off? Likely she will. But I did a terrible thing to Ma and Luli. I probably shouldn't go back there. Chances are Ma will throw me out. Luli won't talk to me. I wouldn't blame them.

I wish I could go straight to Gujiao, but I have no money to get there. And I have to at least warn Luli about Yong. He'll want to get her next.

My mind jumps around like a faulty light bulb with all sorts of thoughts—lost money, fury at Yong, what I should do—but I just keep moving.

By dusk I know I won't make it to Yellow Grain Village tonight. Because of the cold no one is out, so it's easy to slip into a shed that stinks of animals and manure. Several goats are piled together, sleeping. For a moment, I imagine curling up against them for their heat, but I'm too scared to get near them. Instead, I go to a corner and pile straw on top of myself.

Luli would love those goats.

The goats ignore me until just before dawn, when they come over to nudge and sniff at me. I slip out of the shed and continue plodding toward Yellow Grain Village.

CHAPTER 37

Luli

As soon as I step back into Ma's, the pressure of waiting descends on me again.

Mr, Xiang doesn't call or show up all day. I fight with giving up hope. Ma is moody and anxious.

Four more days before I have to return to the factory. I'll have to answer for my absences before the Spring Festival. Bus tickets need to be bought, but I don't know how I can leave Yellow Grain Village if there's no news before then. I listen for sounds in the lane through Ma's rough, wooden walls. I've come to know every drop of a plastic bucket, every cluck of a stray hen, every cough of the old neighbor as he treads to the toilet.

Strangely, I don't hear the footsteps outside before the latch on the handle clunks and the door rasps open. Ma and I both flinch in surprise when Yun comes through and closes the door. She sinks back against it as if she can no longer hold herself up. Her coat is brown with dirt, her face drained deathly white.

Ma and I both jump up.

"You stupid girl! Stupid, stupid!" Ma bolts to Yun and grabs her by the coat. "Where is she? What have you done?"

Yun closes her eyes and turns her face away. She seems to shrink into the door.

Ma squeezes Yun's shoulders until she opens her eyes. "Where's Yong? Where are they?"

Yun swallows dryly. "He took her." Her voice is hoarse and she struggles to get the words out. "Left me when I went to buy her milk."

Ma lets go of her and recoils, a disbelieving, pained expression on her face.

Yun is already turning to me. "Luli, we have to get out of here. He wants to sell you too. When he comes back he's going to try to trick you into going with him, or else just kidnap you outright."

I don't respond—can't speak. My brain can't keep up with what's happening.

"How can you say these things?" cries Ma.

Something flashes in Yun's eyes. "It's the truth! I know he's your son, but this is who he is! This is what he does!" She wheels back toward me, desperate. "Luli, we have to go. We have to get back to the city. We'll both get new jobs so Yong won't know where to find us. We'll blend in with all the other factory girls, and he won't be able to—to—" She looks as if she's on the verge of passing out.

"Enough of this!" Ma snaps. "You're in no shape to go anywhere! And you're talking nonsense. You need to rest." Even now, after everything Yun's put us through, Ma is still trying to take care of her.

"Luli," Yun says.

I take a deep breath. It's not that I don't believe what she's saying about Yong. But I can't leave yet. Not until I hear from Mr. Xiang. I can't give up on Chun yet. "Ma's right," I say to Yun. "You should rest. We'll talk about this more tomorrow."

Yun's whole body sags with exhaustion—with despair.

I debate telling her about Mr. Xiang. I don't know if she cares whether Chun is returned, or if I even care how she feels about it. As for what will happen to her when Mr. Xiang finds out that she helped Yong—I've been torn in half with worry over it, but now I just feel numb. Yun chose to do this. For money, even though I promised to help her pay off the birth fines. For convenience, even though Ma and I would've happily shared the burden of caring for Chun. Yun's world starts and ends with Yun. Mine has revolved around her for too long.

Although I've said that we're like family, a part of me has hardened to her.

Yun staggers toward a chair and buckles into it. "I'm sorry, Ma," she whispers roughly. She turns her eyes to me. "So sorry."

❧ ❧ ❧

The next morning, I see that Yun has crawled into the bed with me. Her hair is flung out, and at the nape of her neck, I can see the thin and bare patches where she's been picking and picking. When I try to climb over her, she wakes up and follows me out of bed. Silently we make Ma tea. Yun helps to set out the cups without my asking. Ma drinks it, and when Yun and I start making breakfast, Ma shoos us out of the way and fixes it herself, her tears falling into the millet soup.

"Luli," Yun says quietly. "Please, can we get a bus to Gujiao today?"

I set my jaw. "I'm still thinking about it."

"But he could—"

"I'm not afraid of him," I cut her off. "And don't worry—I won't hold you responsible if anything bad happens to me. You've made it clear you're not responsible for anyone but yourself."

Yun flinches. The harshness of my own words takes me by surprise, but I don't apologize.

After that, Yun is subdued. Cocooned in her comforter, she sits on the chair in front of the TV, though I won't let her turn it on. Her eyes keep flicking to me. Gradually I feel the anger draining out of me. I can't look at her the same way anymore, but I also can't hate her. It's obvious that she really is sorry for what she's done.

Not that being sorry will bring Chun back.

Maybe nothing will.

I'm still waiting, hoping.

CHAPTER 38

Yun

I hear a car door slam outside Ma's. Luli must have heard the car before I did, because she's at the door and opening it before there's even a knock. Right away she collapses back against the door with a strangled cry.

The next thing I see is Chun's pink blanket with white dots. My hand flies to my mouth.

Ma yelps and darts over, leaving the table and chairs clattering behind her. "My baby!" Tears run fresh down her cheeks as she grabs the baby out of a man's arms and puts her against her shoulder. "You found her! You found her!"

Shock paralyzes me in my chair. Astonishment, relief, and the pressure of the last few days boil up, making me dizzy. I feel as if I might cry too.

I hear the baby whimpering over the noise. My mind reels—*How? Yong? The money!*—but Ma's voice—*Found her, found her!*—rings in my ears.

Chun's mewling begins to get louder, her limbs kicking and thrusting out. Ma turns to shield her from the cold air coming through the door. The man who brought her steps inside, and Luli shuts the door behind him. His broad face and rectangular glasses are familiar to me. Slowly, I place him. The private detective who showed up at Yong's doorstep last year. Xiang, his card read. I stiffen. My hand slips down to gather my blanket tightly around me.

Ma digs her nails into her own cheek. "Where's my boy?"

"Your boy has done an abominable thing," Mr. Xiang says. "Trying to sell this baby to people brokers! His own daughter!"

A hot prickle comes over me. I feel an impulse to jump up and run out the door, but I only grip the armrests of my chair with sweating hands.

"This isn't the first time." Mr. Xiang slaps the back of one hand against the palm of the other and scolds Ma as if she's the one who's guilty. "You know what else he's done."

Ma both shakes and nods her head, twitching in a way that says she knows, but doesn't want to hear it, doesn't want to talk about it. She makes shushing sounds, though whether it's to calm the baby or to hush Mr. Xiang, I'm not sure.

He pulls off his hat and makes a half turn to nod at Luli, before his gaze jumps to me. My heart stops cold. But he only inclines his head before he turns back to Ma.

"Now, in this case, I understand his difficult position—child out of wedlock and all that. He should have married her and set everything right." He juts his chin in my direction. "But if he wasn't going to do it, when the little one is still wanted by one parent, trying to make money from her is just too awful."

Still wanted by one parent? Bewildered, I shoot a look to Luli. She widens her eyes at me and compresses her lips. It's the first time she's really looked at me since I came back. I feel she's trying to tell me something, but I don't understand.

"I told you he was dangerous." Mr. Xiang wags his finger at me. "You're lucky to be rid of him now."

I remember the warning, but I'm puzzled by how he tracked

down Yong. I know better than to ask, although he trains his eyes on me as if waiting for something. A tense, expectant silence hangs in the air beyond Chun's weak cries. Mr. Xiang begins to show lines in his forehead as he studies me. I blink nervously, waiting for him to drag me back to the police station.

Ma, unable to calm Chun, breaks the tension. "When was she last fed?"

"I'll get the bottle!" Luli says loudly. She rushes forward, takes Chun, and crosses over to me. "Just hold her until it's ready," she murmurs, giving me a meaningful look.

I put out my arms. She places Chun in them and darts to the stove. While she's making a racket with pots and bottles, I awkwardly bounce Chun, trying to settle her. Her arms flail, and she makes her feeble but persistent cries. I'm afraid I'll drop her.

"I'm sorry to tell you, but your boy is going to have to take his punishment," Mr. Xiang says to Ma. "I don't know how he got out so quickly last time. Bribery, I'm sure." He clicks his tongue with contempt. "He might have only been an accessory in the previous situation, but this time he's going to be held responsible. Human trafficking! He's going to be charged. A simple greasing of palms won't work for him."

Ma's face is a mash of grief. She backs onto a stool and flops her head onto her arm against the table, sobbing and huffing.

"Don't cry." His sternness falls away. "You can visit him at the Gujiao prison facility."

Ma cries even harder.

"Stop crying, stop crying. There's no use to it." He stands grasping his hat with both hands. "You have this little one to take care of now. That's going to keep you busy enough, eh?"

Mr. Xiang turns his somber face on me again. The two-cell detention center appears in my mind. I shudder, knowing a real prison facility will be much worse. The baby is still uncomfortable in my arms, struggling and making raspy cries, but I'm glad for the weight and bulk of her wrapped in her thick blanket, a buffer as I wait for Mr. Xiang to call me to account.

"You may be required to give a statement," he says to me. "I don't think you'll have to give evidence at the trial since the buyer will be ordered to court. Unless you want to."

My mouth comes open. I draw in breath. I'm trembling again, but for a different reason. He isn't going to have me arrested. He's going to let me off. I bend my head to Chun, shaking so hard she judders in my arms. I'm afraid to say anything in case he changes his mind.

Luli snatches the bottle from the pan of water and brings it over to me. It's barely warm, but I fumble it into Chun's mouth. Luli hovers over me and twists around to Mr. Xiang, a big smile pasted on her face. "Thank you so much for finding Chun!"

She turns to me and hisses into my ear, "Say something!"

Her sharp tone rouses me. "Thank you for getting my daughter back. Thank you so much." My words sound weak and flat even to my own ears. I *am* glad he found Chun—for Ma, for Luli, maybe even for myself—but I'm not sure of the right feelings to show.

"Just let us know what we have to do," Luli says. Her voice is unnaturally loud and bright.

Mr. Xiang puts his hat back on. "I'll be in touch, Miss Cao. For now, I'd better get going." He stands for a moment, looking us over. The moment drags until Ma picks her head up off the table and shows her tear-tracked face. Only now does Mr. Xiang let himself out.

The fake smile drops off Luli's face. She straightens up, hurries to the door, and bolts it with a hard clack.

CHAPTER 39

Luli

After Mr. Xiang leaves, I finally feel like I can breathe. I let out a long, tremulous sigh as I lean against the door, watching Yun with Chun. The baby is sucking furiously at the bottle. Yun is safe from the law, and we're all safe from Yong.

Yun looks so ghostly—ravaged, as bad as when she returned yesterday.

Ma rises and takes Chun from her. "So you came back to us, little one! I hope that wasn't too rough on you," she murmurs to Chun, rubbing her cheek. "Poor thing, taken away from us like that. So lucky he found you."

Yun, sitting sideways in her chair, watches Ma as she paces across the room. Her fingers creep up to her own pale cheek, fingering the pocks on her face, the ones the caretakers at the Institute always told her marked her as unlucky.

"I never believed in luck," she mumbles.

I draw a breath to tell her that she has been lucky today. Lucky that Yong ran out on her before he was caught, that Mr. Xiang didn't notice that she didn't seem like a distraught and grateful mother, that she wasn't arrested.

But I also think of everything that led up to today. All those silent years Yun spent at the Institute. And that one year of making her own choices out in the world, of being able to breathe freely. Over and over again I've told her that everything will be all right, but I've never told her she can have that freedom back. Not anytime soon, at least.

Before I can speak, Ma's head jerks up. "Ha! I know how it is with you!" she snaps. "Just because you were an orphan, you think you can live only for yourself. Hurling forward! Just doing what you want all the time!" She sniffs and takes several strides toward Yun. "But what you don't know is that what you want is right here." She gestures with her hand at all of us. "People. Family." She clicks her tongue. "You've just been too stupid to see it!"

I wince. What Ma says is true—I've been thinking the same thing, after all—but it's not because Yun is stupid.

Ma catches sight of my face. "What? Don't give me that talk about her being broken by the orphanage. I heard you out there yesterday—it's nonsense. She just has the after-birth melancholy. Lots of women get it. She'll be better after her sitting-in month. You young girls don't know anything!"

I want to believe what Ma is saying. That Yun won't always see Chun as a burden, as something trapping her and weighing her down. That in the long run, together, Ma and Yun and I can build a good life—not just for Chun but for us.

I try to catch Yun's eye, but she's studying the blanket draped over her shoulders, fingering the threads.

"You're right about not believing in luck, though," Ma says to Yun. "No one can count on it."

Yun's hand creeps to the nape of her neck. "But can you count on people?" She says it so quietly, I almost don't hear her.

Ma begins to tear up. She turns her back to us. I know she's thinking of Yong. Yun notices too, and by the look on her face, I can tell she feels bad for making Ma cry.

All my anger at her falls away. "Some people you can count on," I say.

She gives me a faint smile, but her gaze drifts to the floor, and she begins plucking out strands of her hair. I can see she's telling herself that *she* can't be counted on, that she isn't ready for Chun, that she isn't good for any baby.

"I know what you're thinking!" I move toward her swiftly to chase away her brooding. "Don't worry about anything! Just get better for now!" I crouch beside her and speak more softly. "This will all work out. Going forward is what matters." Gently, I pull her hands away from her hair. "This much I've learned from you."

CHAPTER 40

Luli

The night before I'm due to go back to the city, Ma's getting ready to do the wash when Yun declares, "I'm going back too. I need to start looking for a new job."

Of course Ma flies into a state. She rails at Yun, says she's too weak to go back now, crazy to even think about it. "You need to start your sitting-in month all over again!"

Yun really doesn't look well. Her face is ashy-white. "I'm fine," she insists, but Ma holds up the pants Yun had been wearing when she walked all those miles home. Blood has soaked through them.

"Does this look fine? Do these pants belong to a girl who can work a full shift without fainting or making herself sick?"

I take Yun aside. "I think you should stay with Ma for now."

Yun bites her lip. "I need to go back to work."

"And you will, soon. Listen, when I get back to Gujiao I'll visit the job center every week and find out which factories are hiring. As soon you're strong enough, I'll help you find a position. We'll work, make money, and come home to visit Chun and Ma every month. The fines will be paid off, I promise. But you have to get stronger first."

Yun doesn't argue. She goes over and picks up Chun, who

isn't even crying. She paces slowly, patting and rocking her, just like Ma does. I can see her heart isn't completely in it. Maybe she's mostly comforting herself. But I think it's also her way of showing that she'll make an effort with Chun—with all of us. And for now, that's enough.

◆◆◆

The bus moves into the thickening traffic near Gujiao. Towering apartment blocks crowd all sides of the crisscrossing expressway, reaching upward and overlapping into the distance until they fade into the brownish smog. I know that behind each of the thousands and thousands of dark windows, a family is housed.

Strangely, the city no longer seems so daunting and lonely. It strikes me that this time I'm the one going ahead and Yun is the one counting on me. Not only Yun, but Chun and Ma as well. They're all counting on me.

I have a strange feeling of lightness as the bus pulls into the station, as if I'm going home.

Author's Note

In 1979, China adopted the One-Child Policy in an effort to control population growth and raise its citizens out of poverty.

The policy had some exceptions allowing second children for ethnic minorities and for rural couples whose first child was a girl or disabled. But for unmarried women and others who became pregnant out of compliance with family planning regulations, the options were to voluntarily abort, be forced to abort, or pay huge fines. Abortion carries no stigma in China, and even late-term abortions are not unheard of. Abortion in China has largely been associated with married women, but the trend of young, single women having abortions, even multiple abortions, is on the rise. Limited sexual education in China means that many young people have little understanding of birth control methods.

Family planning councils could be meticulous with pregnancy checks, charting menstruation and births, coercing abortion and sterilization, and exacting fines. Enforcement of regulations varied widely across the country, but fines for having a baby in violation of regulations could range anywhere from three to ten times a household's annual income. Fines had to be paid for a baby to receive the essential hukou, household registration, which provides access to the most basic social services such as education, healthcare, and legal employment.

In a society with a long-held preference for sons, female babies have often been victims of infanticide or abandonment. After the One-Child Policy went into effect, orphanages became filled with infant girls and disabled children.

The One-Child Policy has created a gender imbalance, about 118 men to 100 women, leaving a surplus of men without enough women for marriage, especially in the countryside. One result is increased human trafficking for brides and prostitution, including the abduction of women from neighboring Vietnam and other South East Asian countries. Children, both boys and girls, are also trafficked for adoption or as future brides.

In 2015, faced with an aging population in a society that relies on the family to support the elder generation, as well as an economy dependent on a massive workforce of cheap labor, the government enacted a Two-Child Policy. Despite the new policy, the newborn birth rate has remained low with many couples citing the rising cost of living and their own positive experiences as singletons as deterrents to having larger families.

In 2018, China's policy-makers have commissioned research studies to consider making more changes, namely eliminating limits and allowing "independent fertility" so a family could decide how many children they will have.

Acknowledgments

I am so lucky to have fallen in with P. B. Parris, Ann Howell, Linda Steitler, and Williamaye Jones. You have all been so giving and patient. We all know how much you have helped with this story from the very beginning and beyond.

Thank you to Chung Liu, D.L. Ellenburg, Virginia Pye, my mother Mei-jy Liu, and Jane Lee for reading the manuscript and giving thoughtful feedback or helping me to find answers to my many questions. Nathan, Alex and Eliot Boniske, thank you for all kinds of support and space you've provided so I could do this.

Shannon Hassan, agent and Amy Fitzgerald, editor, you both awe me with your whip-like smartness and how well you do your work. I greatly appreciate you both for taking on *Girls on the Line* and helping to make it a much finer novel.

Topics for Discussion

1. What characteristics make Luli and Yun different from each other? How have their different experiences in early childhood shaped their personalities?

2. What does family mean to Luli? What does it mean to Yun?

3. Why does Yun initially dismiss Ming's warning about Yong? What role does jealousy play in various characters' behavior throughout the novel?

4. Describe some cultural attitudes toward orphans in China. How do these attitudes affect Luli's and Yun's opportunities and the way they see themselves?

5. Contrast Dali's plans for her future with Luli's. Why do you think Luli has such different aspirations?

6. What are some differences between China and the United States in terms of family planning policies and options? What are some differences in cultural attitudes toward abortion, pregnancy out of wedlock, and motherhood?

7. Why does Yun have no desire to be a mother? How does she express this?

8. How do laws and money affect Yun's decisions about her pregnancy? How do people around her influence her actions?

9. Why is Luli so determined to help Yun keep the baby instead of taking the baby to the orphanage? What is she overlooking in her eagerness to take care of Yun and the baby?

10. According to his family, how has Yong's life been influenced by his lack of a hukou? Do you believe Ma's claim that all Yong's problems and bad decisions stem from this?

11. Why does Yun decide to help Yong sell Chun? How does she justify this decision to herself? What are her alternatives and why does she dismiss them?

12. When Yun leaves with Yong and Chun, she reflects, "People have often let me know that I'm a worthless person, but now I feel I'm a terrible one." Why does she feel this way? Do you agree? Why or why not?

13. What are Ming's motivations? In what ways has his behavior toward Luli throughout the novel been manipulative or controlling? What red flags has Luli noticed, and what has she missed?

14. After Yun and Yong leave with Chun, how does Luli feel about Yun's actions? What eventually moves Luli to forgive Yun for her actions?

15. What do you think Chun's life will be like? Do you think she will be better off than Luli, Yun, and Yong were? Why or why not?

16. At the end of the novel, what do you think the characters would change about their situations? How do you think their experiences in the novel will influence their choices in the future?

UNEXPECTED.
ECLECTIC.
ADVENTUROUS.

For more distinctive and award-winning YA titles, reader guides, book excerpts, and more, visit *CarolrhodaLab.com.*

Follow Lerner on social media!

About the Author

Jennie Liu is the daughter of Chinese immigrants. Having been brought up with an ear to two cultures, she has been fascinated by the attitudes, social policies, and changes in China each time she visits. She lives in North Carolina with her husband and two boys. Follow her at jennieliuwrites.com or on Twitter @starnesliu.